DIVIDED
A BROKEN REALMS NOVELLA

T.J. FISHER

Edited by
REBECCA CRAIG

DIVIDED

Published 2023 Broken Realms Publications
Copyright © 2024 by T.J. Fisher
All rights reserved.
Paperback ISBN: 978-1-7329150-4-6

No part of this book may be reproduced in any form or by any electronic or mechanical means, including information storage and retrieval systems, without written permission from the author, except for the use of brief quotations in a book review.

Mom,
*You made me believe in the
idea that animals could talk.*

CONTENTS

1. Irigiim — 1
2. Castell — 6
3. Irigiim — 13
4. Castell — 19
5. Irigiim — 25
6. Castell — 31
7. Irigiim — 37
8. Castell — 43
9. Irigiim — 48
10. Castell — 53
11. Irigiim — 59
12. Castell — 65
13. Irigiim — 72
14. Castell — 79
15. Irigiim — 86
16. Castell — 91
17. Irigiim — 99
18. Castell — 103
19. Irigiim — 108
20. Castell — 113
21. Irigiim — 116
    Review — 123

    Reference & Pronunciation Guide — 125
    Acknowledgments — 131
    About the Author — 133
    Also by T.J. Fisher — 135

CHAPTER 1

IRIGIIM

My pup slashes at the air. A squall of legs and arms as she twists, pretending to sever or maybe stab a supposed enemy, a tight grip on the knives in her hands. I can never tell the difference between the many fighting forms, the human shape is still relatively unknown to me, even though Rayle took the time to explain the katas. She is dedicated, as she should be for a Stieti Tetsaa. It is one of the many attributes I admire and why I chose her to be my partner, but honestly, it makes little sense to me to attack something that is not there. As a wolf, all my actions have purpose. Why humans determine it necessary to keep practicing with their sharp objects is beyond me. Once my play sessions from puppyhood turned into real hunts with teeth and claws, everything I did from then on was instinctual. I do not understand why it is not the same for the Isokanii people. In my brief time bonded to Rayle, I recognize that, for her, the fighting sequences are a means to help her focus a bundle of energy. My partner reminds me so much of myself as a puppy exploring outside the safety of the den for the first time.

She is not timid and shy, but she seems fascinated by the smallest things. I should not be so harsh in my critiques. I, too, was a pup once, discovering the whipping quiddity of new branches, but that was many years ago.

Rayle does a pretty flip and twists through the air to give a hard chop toward her imagined enemy. The stone and wooden beads in her hair clatter as the long, thin braids settle into stillness across her back and over her shoulder. The riot of colors in the filtered light interests me. Purple opals intertwined with copper and silver wire around the crown of her head impress her status as royalty among the Isokanii, but the addition of blue, yellow, and red wooden beads is uniquely Rayle. Her final pose gives her a very cat-like quality as she spreads her legs low and wide. I wonder at the difficulty of keeping her head aloft with the extra weight from the beads, but then again, I wonder at how any human moves at all with only two thin legs to propel them.

I tilt my head, twitching an ear forward as I listen to the steadying of her breath. Rayle told me a few days ago that the long pause at the end of her practice is so she can pray to the gods. I do not believe in her gods, but I suppose our bonding—on the dark moon a few days ago—would now allow me to find out more, but the connection between us is still more ghostly than tangible, and I often forget it is there. Perhaps more so due to hesitation in the face of the unknown than any true obstacle.

I unblock the mental link between us and, sure enough; she is praying to Jurana, the goddess of the sun. I should ask later why she chooses that goddess in particular to venerate with her prayers. My pup's thoughts differ vastly from my own, they are wild and untamable. She will think of one thing and then be on to the next before the first is finished, never committing to one idea or thought for long. The only thing that seems to focus her attention are the sword and dagger practices, and these she does with unbridled determination and concentration. So far, my conclusions about humans have settled between complicated and messy. Still, I look upon her with fondness.

My world—at least before the pup—consisted of eating, sleeping, wandering beneath soaring trees while socializing with my brethren, and hunting. It was a simple life, and I liked it. Though the generalities of my life before mirrored that of the lowly insipid creatures that resemble my kind but have the mental complexity of a frightened rabbit; I was capable of more than living a life of basic urges. We Beast are intelligent and thoughtful creatures, able to communicate on a higher level than any other animals in existence. It is why we have the ability to choose partnership with the royal family of the Isokanii, like I did with Rayle. It is a position of power I relish.

Bonding, however, limits me in some aspects, but I do not regret my choice. The advantages I gain in spite of this uncomfortable transition period—my skin still spasms and itches—are worth the price. I now understand human speech, and with it, a seemingly endless list of words to describe the complexity of an object or situation. Something I find to be a pleasant challenge as I translate my native Beast communication to new descriptors, even if I stumble over an apt word or phrase from time to time. I have learned the Isokanii language quickly because of my bond, but sometimes when I try to use the appropriate words to speak with Rayle, they stick in my mind like an old dried piece of game between my teeth. My pup always has a laugh at my expense in those moments, which frustrates me, but Rayle assures me that with time I will taste the marrow of words' usefulness.

Bonding also ensures my survival. The Sun Dwellers, for the past twenty-some-odd years for unknown reasons, have hunting fever, like the lesser animals who lust to bite something with their white-foam mouths. The selfish mages covet the abilities of my kin. Since our discovery, I have seen several of my brethren murdered. I cannot recall how many Beast have been ripped from this realm into the other, sentenced to a life of abasement and horror. It both angers and frightens me to know they are used merely for mindless killing. I bonded so I would not be one of them. My sire never liked the idea of bonding with a human and always discouraged the pack from doing so. He often compared it to being alone and cornered for the rest of existence. What my sire did not foresee was his demise because of his staunch position on freedom. If he was still alive, I like to think he would understand the advantages of bonding, but antecedently, I would have followed his lead and remained wild. Our numbers dwindle every day because of the Sun-Dwelling mages, and other than siring more Pups, this is the only way to preserve my kind. Sure, my life-span reduces to that of my partner's, and I will only live for another sixty or seventy years, but I keep my sanity, and I remain, mostly, my own master, since a bonded Beast cannot become a puppet to the defilers in the other realm.

So far, my bond with Rayle feels nothing like being cornered. Granted, it has only been a few days, but she thus far treats me with respect and kindness, and I foresee a camaraderie between us that will deepen our tender friendship. She is a handful. I hear many attribute this description to her nature, but I picked her during the Ermyjek Ceremony because she is strong both in spirit and body. If I am going to attach my life to a human, I want one that will not dart from danger like my meals.

Rayle's movement pulls me from my thoughts as she rises from her deep position and turns to give me a big grin. I snort my approval at her regimen. I may not understand the incessant practicing, but she *is* one of the best fighters amongst the Chausekki family. My choice of partner is a good one.

"Irigiim," Rayle says, "I was thinking we should explore the other realm when it is full night. Now that we are bonded, I can finally open pathways to explore!"

'No.'

"Irigiim, do not be like that. The full night there is when all the Sun Dwellers are sleeping and you are a big, strong male and can protect me."

I bare my teeth at the taunt. *'My answer is still no. Why should either of us put ourselves in harm's way when those mages are acting like nothing more than selfish pups, all trying to share the same teat? They need to act more like a pack.'*

Rayle lets out a huff. "Fine."

I flatten my ears and give her a small growl. I do not know Rayle well enough yet to know if she will keep her word, but I figure a minor threat does not hurt.

She is nonplussed.

"Well, if you will not go to the other realm, at least venture with me to the quarries after the wedding. I have always wanted to see them."

Unease trickles through me, but the link I share with my wild brethren indicates no lurking, foul smells or sounds in that area. I see no harm in visiting the quarries as long as we remain in the Shade Realm. If we keep closer to the Eastern edge, we will be away from the primary conflict along the river. I obviously do not worry about being pulled, but it is better to be safe than sorry. Rayle seems to have a propensity to find her way into sticky situations, that is what my gut tells me. I snap my teeth at my pup, still somewhat irritated by her request, but she can feel my intentions. A smile blooms across her face. I like this display of happiness. The energy pleases me, making my acquiescence worth her happiness.

CHAPTER 2
CASTELL

Several more hours of this drudgery, he thought, after peeking at the position of the sun; and he didn't even have the midday break to look forward to because it already passed.

Castell sank onto his heels from his hunched position with a burdened sigh. Using a small burst of wind, he cleared away the dust from the rock he'd been chiseling. Could he have used the brush sitting next to him? Yes, but that didn't provide a refreshing breeze to give him a respite from the blazing sun. Castell squinted at the burning orb as he removed his large scrub grass hat and wiped away the sweat threatening to drip into his eyes. Why couldn't he have been an Amber mage like his brother? They had it so much easier here at the mines, being able to sense the metals and minerals in the ground. They could shift the earth to soften it and simply pull the Sun Crystal formations from the rock. Those workers, by far, had the highest collection count of anyone else and were paid the most. It was useless to complain, though; no one chose their gift from the gods. At least he could summon light breezes to keep himself cool while the brutal sun lashed at his back. That was infinitely preferable to constantly sucking in the arid radiant heat intent on slowly baking everything.

The hard stone of the quarries, with its ever-present dusting of dirt, was not his choice for a living location, but Castell had lived here his entire life with his parents and siblings; he knew nothing else. More than once he'd daydreamed about living under the cool canopy of a forest with soft loam under his feet, like from the stories his father told. The longer he was a resident of the quarries, the more he questioned his reasons for staying.

Of course, it was the thought of his family that usually subdued the itch to leave. What would he do without family dinners on the sixth moon each week where he played hide-and-seek with his youngest sister, or threw good-natured punches at his brother? His family and friends were content with the life they'd made here, but for years now Castell felt his life would be better lived somewhere else. Which again begged the question: why did he continue to stay?

What good was a weather mage to a quarry? Sure, he could provide cloud cover or create breezes to make workers more comfortable, but he certainly didn't provide any useful contributions of Sun Crystal to the foreman each evening.

Did he stay because of his reliance on familiarity?

The only thing in his entire life he counted as useful was work with the other Weathers to summon showers so crops grew in excess in this desert highland. He supposed creating storms and rain wasn't entirely useless, but that work only happened for a portion of the year and their small settlement didn't need eight Weathers to complete the tasks needed for growing crops. His presence and talents were in excess. What really was stopping him?

Castell looked around him. To his right his father chiseled at a crystal, and he could hear the faint hum of *Beneath the Canopy*. It was a song Castell heard often over the years, and his father once admitted he sang it because it reminded him of his childhood home. On a higher rocky outcropping, his brother too chiseled at a crystal, but his movements were aggressive, as if he could simply coerce the stone to give up its prize instead of gently removing the layers. His father and brother were far enough away that he couldn't talk to them, but at least they were there, always in range for a shout or breezed message. Would it be their presence he missed if he left?

If I found a life somewhere else, I would be completely alone.

Leaving here would come with a huge amount of loss. Could he actually handle that kind of breakaway? Tucking an errant strand of his sun-lightened brown hair behind his ear—he really needed another trimming—Castell replaced his hat and set his chisel to the stone once more. Light taps flaked the bleached shale around the base of the Sun Crystal.

But should my fear prevent me from living a life I might enjoy? I would hate staying here for the rest of my life, that is certain. If I join the war I could put my gift to better use. Yes?

Leaving was a question he'd contemplated for months. He'd hesitated between staying and going. Life in Sun Glimmer was familiar and comfortable, but he also wasn't happy. He needed to decide. Stay or go? A simple question with a complicated answer.

He could be an asset to the war effort. Spending hours at a time maintaining breezes for himself and others had made him a strong mage. Those with exceptional gifts were always wanted, right? Maybe that was his own justification, since he had no formal schooling thanks to his parents' beliefs, but Castell felt he could hold his own against at least a Prime Mage, a Cleric classification. It was his estimate. The majority of the castings he knew now were niche, designed specifically to benefit Sun Glimmer.

Maybe, given the proper knowledge, he could work castings better suited to war. But what would his parents think of him leaving to join a decades long conflict?

His parents would hate his decision.

Every resident of the quarry kept discussion of the war hush, and his parents were no exception. Questions or comments that could start even a flicker of a debate were snuffed. Out here, no one wanted to be involved with the fighting, even though they still craved the latest news of the conflict. What was it with people who wouldn't fight but still opined on something? That alone made leaving to join the war more appealing. At least his magic could be used for something more than mundane tasks. What Castell didn't know—because no one would tell him—was which side he should support. That was the problem of living with pacifists.

He agreed that the fighting should stop. It was doing nothing for their society or the land, but he wanted to know which faction would bring about the best changes.

If there was such a thing as winning in war.

The most recent merchant caravan brought news that the battles along the great river had become worse. Each side gathered more and more followers, making the war a constant tug of back and forth between sides. The news of a once lush area now barely clinging to survival had saddened his father.

The most hated side from overheard conversations in the tavern, and the one often blamed to have started the war, were The Clerics; and those allegedly justified in their retaliation were The Purists. The Clerics believed a centralized system of government should be in place where the strongest mages filled the more prominent ranks. The Purists believed that the way life had been for hundreds of years—groups of people living as they wished with their own government structures—should remain untouched. In Purist living, information passed from older mages to the younger, and every once in a while, a new spell was discovered. The information was then given to traders and passed around to other settlements. Clerics wanted people to always push the limits of their understanding, studying to gain mastery with ruthless zeal. Castell did question the Clerics' ideologies when the ways of Purists had worked for so many generations. What really did they gain from their system? No one he knew had an answer nor wanted to answer his question.

Right now, not knowing which side to support was the major reason preventing him from leaving his small community. It was a tough decision to make. On the one hand, there was something redeemable in a planned, standardized structure of government that had balance, but he did question why the most *powerful* mages should be the ones in charge and decide things. Just because he was a strong Weather Mage didn't mean he should be the quarry's foreman. Here in Sun Glimmer, no one cared about your magical strength. Everything of importance was debated by those who had seen at least twenty summers or more, which was most of the settlement. Decisions often took weeks, if not months, to make collectively. He'd been a part of every one of the Fire Talks for six summers now and he hated them, even if they were necessary. There seemed to be a constant lack of keenness to move through the agenda. It frustrated him.

Despite his lack of enthusiasm for the meetings, Castell recognized the value of multiple voices being heard. His father was an Indigo Mage, using his gift to tell complex stories with detailed illusions. But that didn't mean he should be automatically overruled by someone just because they were more powerful.

Castell scrunched his face. Why couldn't there be some type of compromise? Designing a hierarchical rating system could help magic-users know where they could put their skills to use more efficiently, but that system did not have to come with dogmatic rules. Did it? From what his parents had told him, sharing all knowledge had been the basis of society until the Clerics, born out of a group who created the Magic School System, sought control.

Frustration surged in Castell and he huffed out a breath. All of his knowledge still brought him back to the question of what he should do about it. Should he follow the path of his parents and remain an uncertain pacifist? Should he join the Purists? The Clerics? Which choice would bring back some semblance of normalcy? What was normal? If the Fire Talks taught him anything, it was that 'normal' meant something different to each person.

Castell threw his tools to the ground in front of him, which made Olke perk her large ears. He reached over and scratched the small fox. The attention had her crawling into his lap with a flick of her black-tipped tail. Castell smiled at the little fox, no bigger than the length of his forearm. He'd found Olke as a kit abandoned and terrified in one of the many tunnels of the quarry, her sandy fur mud-caked. She'd cried in fear with her warbling chirp each time she saw him before he'd given her enough food to show that he was trustworthy. Now Olke was an inseparable companion. Many didn't understand why he kept company with one of the many predators roaming the quarries, but Castell couldn't let her starve. He knew the way of things in the wild. Animals died all the time without the intervention of mages. He had just chosen for it to not be this one.

Olke's affection made him feel better, but it didn't distract him. The manual labor of the quarry did nothing to improve his thoughts, and right now, anything looked more appealing than the work in front of him, even the war. He, of course, needed to finish chiseling this Sun Crystal before he could retire for the day. Castell retrieved his chisel and hammer. Striking the rock, he concluded he needed information. He would only get it by confronting his parents. In the past, they'd scarcely mentioned the war and their reasons for fleeing. Now their silence wasn't a good enough answer. If he was going to make a proper decision, he needed his parents to talk about the war, and he would do it tonight. The topic would pain them because it had uprooted their lives, but Castell no longer wanted to live in ignorance or passivity. He might agree with some of his parents' ideals, but living noncommittally would not cut it for him anymore.

CHAPTER 3
IRIGIIM

Another tingle creeps along my spine. This is the fifth time it's happened, and I cannot figure out why I feel squirmy, especially at an event so mundane and dull. Usually, my muscles only twitch this much when hunting. Nothing about this ceremony is anticipatory. In fact, Rayle told me this was to be a joyous occasion. I took her word for it since this was the first human ceremony I have witnessed besides the one used for the Ermyjek Ceremony. I did not want to, but I conceded to myself that I had been intrigued to see what the excitement was all about for this wedding. Now that I am here, I find myself rather puzzled by the whole affair. Why the spread of tail feathers when the mate selection was years ago? There is no need for displays of superiority at this point. I truly do not see why this wedding is necessary.

Colorful fabrics hang criss-cross in relaxed arches along the open-air ceiling and fragrant rose petals allude to an aisle in the middle of the gathered Beast and Isokanii. The thick purple, blue, and green swaths mostly block the sun streaming into the throne room in the late day, but the heat is still intense enough for servants to circulate the stifling afternoon swelter with large palms. I suppose all the finery combined with the effects of the textiles and bedded floral aisle is grand enough, but I still do not see the point.

At the steps of the dais below the massive gilded throne are the two Isokanii we are here to celebrate, a man called Kaalak and a woman called Serrett—Rayle's eldest sister. From what my pup tells me, Serrett is also a great fighter, which is why she is marrying the first son of the second prince. She officially won his hand after her victory in the d'Kehbzi where she slew her opponent. I think this is at odds with what Rayle said about the two being a slated pair for many years prior, but apparently, the Isokanii believe the value of a woman lies in how well she can defend. She says the man defends the woman and, in turn, the woman defends the home, children, and her man, when necessary. So, if Serrett lost to her challenger, she would currently be the one buried in the royal gardens. I glance at the parents of the girl who lost and there is no joy to be found on either of their faces, but their royal blood requires them to be here. All of it seems unbalanced, needlessly brutal and unfair to me. However, the Isokanii believe it is a command from the gods as a way to keep the realm balanced. Since I do not share their faith, who am I to question it?

Prior to the ceremony, Rayle confided that she did not want to be here since she rarely relates with Serrett. Her sister is very much her opposite in personality because she prefers to always be pristine—Rayle's derisive word—while my bond partner does not mind a little dirt caking her skin. My pup is not *dirty*; I will not let her be. She simply is not particular. It is this particularity that creates such a sizable gap between them in addition to the eight-year age difference. I glance around again, and the decorations certainly lend to the idea of pristine. I am seeing why Rayle said she often struggles to be civil with her kin.

Another shiver inches its way down my spine, making me shift uneasily. I try to do it as subtly as possible, but, being the grand creature I am, subtlety isn't easy.

'This is your first royal function, Irigiim? You seem most unsettled.' Shurra, the lithe little fox Beast next to me, catches my eye. She is still large compared to the Isokanii, but as a fox she is one of the smaller Beasts roaming the realm. She would still be a formidable opponent, though, and I unquestionably do not want to pit myself against her wisdom and experience.

'Yes, but I find this affair bromidic. I do not know why I am so shifty,' I reply.

Shurra's amusement comes across our mental link. *'I cannot say I disagree, but I think, in this instance, it is your partner making you so. Rayle, yes?'*

I nod.

'She has been shifty the entire ceremony.'

I specifically focus on my partner and, sure enough, Rayle is subtly shifting from foot to foot. *'I did not realize our connection would affect me in this way.'*

'You are just bonded? I heard there had been a ceremony on the last dark moon.'

'Yes.'

Shurra is amused at me again. I dislike her teasing nature. She certainly feels my displeasure, but does nothing to temper her delight. *'Do not be so vexed. I too was once in your position, thirty or so years ago. Your bond is still new, but you will get used to each other's feelings soon enough, and you will learn how to block most of it so it does not overwhelm you as much.'*

She was not unkind, but her words still chastised me. I may be centuries old, but my wisdom does not yet extend to life as a partner of a Stieti Tetsaa. It would be cretinous not to heed her words.

'I do apologize, Shurra, you of course, are more versed in the ways of being bonded than I am.'

'Think nothing of it, Irigiim,' she says with a flick of her tail. *'I would be happy to discuss it more during the feast if you wish for the company.'*

'Indeed.'

A wash of relief sweeps through me, and I return my attention to the ceremony, now ecstatic that it is finally over; or is that Rayle's feelings filtering into me? My pup explained that attendants, like she is for her sister, are unnecessary and not common, but fulfilling the role was important to Serrett; and despite their frequent disdain for one another, my pup does care for her sister. Either way, it is over. At least we can move on to the food.

Rayle crawls over my crossed legs and falls against my chest, disappearing into my luxurious obsidian fur. I fully open my mind to our link and my partner is very moody from being made to stand still for so long. It has made her feel exhausted, and I can feel her desperation to escape to a training yard. Except it is time for the feast and she is expected to sit with her family.

I do my best to console her. *'It is only for a short time, and not much to ask for one day.'*

"No," she replies, her lips pursed petulantly.

'But...'

"Still does not mean I have to like it."

'You think I enjoy such a jejune affair? This very human custom is ridiculous to me.'

Rayle groans. "I know, Irigiim. I am sorry you have to be here, but it is simply part of being born into the Family Chausekki." She says this last part as if quoting something she has heard a hundred times.

'At least next there is food,' I say.

"Of course you are excited about the food. Always hungry."

'That is not true, but I cannot deny the pleasure of being served my weight in raw meat. Even if I cannot eat all of it. I enjoy being revered.'

"Do not let it go to your head."

'I appreciated the veneration long before I bonded to you, pup. Just wait, you will learn to appreciate it one day too now that you are amongst an elite group, thanks to me.'

"I doubt it. I just want to be free from this ceremony."

'And we will be... after the feast.'

Rayle groans again, but she pushes away from my chest. Grudgingly, she crawls back over my leg and makes her way to the royal gardens where the feast is being presented. At least we will be outside, which I much prefer to the semi-enclosed space of the royal buildings. I push myself up and follow Rayle to the gardens, the smell of Jasmine rising on the breeze and making my nose twitch.

The garden really is a lovely place. In the distance is the large body of water that forms an oasis around which the Isokanii built their capital. Buildings in the city blend into the rich flora, but the royal palace is a monstrosity of stone in comparison because it must house so many Beasts. The tranquility of the gardens reminds me a lot of the still places in the forest—which, like Rayle, I am eager to return to.

My pup and I part ways since the seating for the humans has low hanging lanterns and fabrics. Any Beast is simply too large to lounge in such a space. I settle next to Shurra behind a square tile. I place my paw on it, letting the refreshing cool soak through into my pads. To the Isokanii, this grassless space is massive, taking them a little over twelve human steps to go from the left-to-right corner, but to me it is only slightly larger than my paw. I am barely comfortable before food is being piled in front of me. The meat of the skinned animals includes everything from large birds—the ones with long legs that run quickly and are fun to chase—to muscle laden reptiles. The fare is a departure from what I normally consume in the forest, but it fills me the same. I could be picky, and the Isokanii would go out of their way to accommodate me, but as long as my belly remains full I really do not care about what exactly is filling it.

After a few mouthfuls I say to Shurra, *'So, tell me more about what it is like to be bonded.'*

CHAPTER 4
CASTELL

"Ama, Papa, I have a question for you." Castell said, not long after sitting for dinner. The small wooden chair made his knees awkwardly close to the underside of the table, but the comfort of the familiar made it bearable. Remote life didn't lend itself to getting new materials easily, so his father had continued to repair the chairs since he was a child, yet those repairs didn't stop the legs from being rubbed shorter and shorter as it scraped along the stone floor.

Tonight he could have eaten alone at his home, but because he did not have a household of his own, his mother often invited him to dine with them outside of their more formal family meals. Staying home would have ensured a drama free evening, yet here he sat, ready to poke the bee's hive. A soft crunch from Olke crackled about the cavern kitchen as she curled happily beneath his chair, munching on a few raw eggs his mother set into a clay bowl.

"What is that?" His father, Siggri, said between a bite of his roasted brush hen.

Castell pushed at his cinnamon yams as nerves coursed through him, but if he wanted answers, he needed to plunge ahead into the bitter subject of the war. "Why did you and Ama leave and not stay to fight in the war?"

Silence settled over the dining and kitchen space, so heavy he heard an owl's call outside before it swooped to catch prey.

"What has made you curious about such a topic?" Pleasa, his mother, responded in her usual soft, cautious tone.

Castell shrugged, attempting to show less interest than he felt. He had to approach this conversation with great care, otherwise his parents would seal their lips, never to speak of it again, especially in front of his little sister. Tiecia had grown up in a world with few mentions of war and none of them so direct as their discussion now. His parents talked of it less and less as the years progressed, since it affected them little and there appeared to be no resolution in sight. "It is just that what I have heard from the traders as they pass through makes it sound like the war is not going so well."

"That is because war has no good resolution," Siggri responded sternly. "It is two sides that cannot agree, but fighting is no way to settle disputes. We have raised you to know that."

"Yes, and I agree, fighting does not solve the issue, but that is not really answering my first question. Why did you leave your home in the forest?"

"The fighting was too close to our home, love," Pleasa said. "We wanted you to grow up safe and without constant fear."

That made sense. Castell, for a moment, tried to imagine what he would have done if he had been in his parents' shoes. Would he have wanted his own child to grow up amidst battles and strife? No, but part of him resented his parents for taking a coward's path and running as far from the fighting as possible. Castell wasn't naïve enough to believe that two people alone could change the course of the future. Or could they? Could he? Maybe. He'd seen it often, even in his small village of Sun Glimmer, how one man with enough influence could turn the course of people's thoughts.

How different would his life have been if his parents hadn't fled to this remote settlement in the quarries? Would he have joined the war already? This was his twenty-sixth summer, and the war had been active for twenty-five. It's possible that he could have died many seasons ago. His parents' action certainly led to him living for this many seasons. Yet, could he call this a living? Ignoring the current state of the world and simply waiting for an outcome, waiting for one side to be victorious?

"I understand," Castell began slowly, "and I am grateful, but do you not have some opinion on the justification of the Clerics versus the Purist?" Castell hoped he was not pushing the subject too far.

"No, Castell, you know what happens when someone fights for their own justification," Siggri said. "The war has gone on for your entire life and nothing has been resolved. No one has won anything. The only thing this war has provided is ruin. Ruin of homes and of lives, and both sides are eternally responsible for that."

"But why do we say that both sides are wrong? The Clerics believe they have just cause to fight and the Purists believe the same. We believe neither should fight at all. In the end, what good is anyone doing in this war?"

His parents' faces turned to stone. Not surprising since he had challenged their beliefs.

"Ama, what is a war?" Tiecia asked in the silence.

Pleasa patted her daughter's hand. "Do you remember the times Castell and Averek have been angry with one another? Shouting?"

"Mmm hmm."

"Well, war is just like that, but with more people and more serious consequences."

Castell bit the inside of his cheek to keep from saying something rude to his mother. It was just like her to use him and Averek as an example of how not to act. He understood why she did it. He and his brother were years older than his little sister and they should be examples, but it still irritated him, especially because she did it in the middle of an important conversation.

Siggri fixed him with a narrow gaze and said, "Do you believe you could sway this war one way or the other? Are you the one to change the course of the future?"

The question caught him off guard. Castell set down his fork to give full attention to his father. "I do not know, but sitting here waiting for an outcome does not seem like the right answer."

"Love, where is this coming from? You have been quiet about the war your entire life," Pleasa said, a mixture of sadness and bewilderment coloring her voice.

"I have just been thinking."

Castell took a bite of his food, ignoring his parents' concerned gaze. He didn't know where this thought had come from. Unhappiness in his work and overhearing the traders at the inn probably started the ideas rolling. With nothing to do but the mindless task of chiseling away stones, it was easy to let the thoughts mature. Before his time spent at the inn, he'd always relied on his parents for updates on the war, even if it was the smallest bit of information. Listening to the traders in the lower settlement had been his first time hearing the news firsthand. Maybe that had been it. Maybe not hearing about the war through his parent's filter had been the spark igniting the fast-growing desire inside of him.

"Love, I beg you to let these ideas go. They will only eat you up inside, and you can do nothing about the war from here. That is why we moved here with the rest of our neighbors."

"Then maybe I should leave so I can do something about it."

Castell had tried to say it gently, but it came out sharper than he'd intended. His mother's gasp and his father's frown said everything, and shock was just the beginning of it. His mother pulled his little sister from her chair to hold her close and shelter her from such outrageous ideas. Tiecia squirmed at the sudden confinement.

"You cannot mean that," Pleasa said pleadingly.

Castell clenched his jaw and turned his face away from her pained one. "I am not sure."

"Son, joining a war is no life to live."

"And digging at rocks all day is?"

"It is a simple life, but it is free of worry. If you had married years ago, had a child, perhaps you would not be dissatisfied with your lot in life," Siggri said.

Oh no, we will not have that argument again, Pappa.

"I cannot accept that. You,"—he pointed at his father—"are a powerful mage. Your illusions could have potentially saved thousands of lives."

"Son, it—"

"You, mother," Castell turned his accusation to her, "your knowledge of the human body and how to mend it could have also been of help, regardless of what side you chose."

Pleasa placed a hand over his sister's ears, pressing her lips into a fine line as tears welled in her eyes.

"Do not speak to your mother that way, Castell. Your mother would have likely been forced to hurt people with her gift, and I the same. We were not willing to live a life of slavery disguised as freedom, *hoping* to stop a war. No, we would rather stay out of the fighting than betray ourselves and all we value."

Castell hadn't considered what negative things his parents might have been forced to do. "I need some time to think." Shoving away from the table, Castell picked up Olke and pushed the heavy curtain separating the main tunnel from their living quarters with more force than necessary. "And some fresh air."

The air outside would just be beginning to cool, and it was much better than the stale, semi-smokey air inside the network of tunnels housing the residents of his village. He made the necessary turns to the exit. Maybe his father was correct, maybe his dissatisfaction did come from not building a life here. Hopefully, summoning a fresh breeze to refresh his lungs would blow away his resentful thoughts.

Hopefully, but he doubted it.

CHAPTER 5
IRIGIIM

'We *already discussed this, Rayle. You are not going to the Sun Realm just to satisfy your curiosity,'* I said, irritated that we were on this subject for the third time within the span of seven suns.

"I understand you are concerned, Irigiim, but exploration is what it means to be a Stieti Tetsaa."

'You have used that argument before and it has yet to convince me. There is nothing wrong with leading a simple life and protecting your people. I know from your memories that your instructor Eniila told you as much.'

My pup crinkles her nose, annoyed at my obstinance. I slightly bare my teeth. It is a mutual feeling.

"Since you have seen my memories, then you know I did not agree with instructor Eniila. It is our job to protect the tribes, and if we do not know the state of the current war and what is unfolding, then we are neglecting a significant portion of our duties," Rayle counters. "Besides, as a Stieti Tetsaa, they have given me weapons to help protect me from magic"—she held up her sword and dagger, beautiful curved things with wicked edges and obsidian crystals in the hilt—"and you Irigiim are immune to magic."

I quiet for a moment, considering what she said. Although my pup does not know it, I too attended a class of sorts in order to prepare myself for the experience of bonding with my partner. Not that I will ever tell her this since all Isokanii believe us to be perfect. I will maintain that facade for as long as possible. Besides, Gaipanii only taught us these things because he wished to help us understand our new status and situation. The Beast, bonded with Rayle's instructor for nearly fifty years, knew what to communicate for me to be as equipped as possible for the ceremony. During my brief time under his guidance, I learned protecting the tribes would be the primary function of my existence.

At first, I recoiled at being made so low, into a mere sentry, but I soon understood it to be a great honor and something we should look forward to for it provided the opportunity to expand our understanding of the world. If I am willing to admit it, a small part of me wanted to bond because of a desire to learn more about the world despite the love of my independence and forest home.

Not for the sake of satisfying my curiosity, since it is such a fickle emotion, but I want to know more about the magicians of the Sun Realm that imprison and destroy my brethren. Perhaps the exploration will help me identify ways to save them from such a horrible fate.

"I see you, Irigiim, licking your lips. I have convinced you." Rayle says.

For the love of Beast, my pup did just convince me to join her on an exploration. I'm not happy with my capitulation. It is a defeat, and I hate losing. I am ever fearful of what could happen while in the other realm.

'You do not feel the changes in the realm as one of my brethren becomes enslaved to the other side. If I am close enough, I can feel the malicious intent of the magic every time they are carried away. I am uneasy walking into such a realm and so should you be,' I reply, one final attempt to sway her to my way of thinking.

"You are the most cowardly Beast I have ever come across!" She pushes her hands in my direction as she stalks away.

I assume the gesture was meant to be dismissive or convey her disgust, the emotion trickling between our link has the heat of a fresh kill. There is a lot I will look past because my pup is so young; insolence, I am unwilling to let go. Rayle needs to learn right now that I will not tolerate her irascible attitude or be pushed around so easily in the future. I want to snap my jaws to see her jump, but I temper my anger. With a single step, I block her path easily with my snout and peel back my lips for her to see my gleaming teeth, made white by the bones I use to scrape them clean. Turning so one of my eyes is as close to her as possible, I give a low growl and say, *'If you wish to remain in my good graces, I suggest you do not call me a coward ever again.'*

Rayle's body language is more startled than afraid at my posturing, but she also has the good sense to look repentant. "I am sorry, Irigiim." She sighs. "I am just frustrated, and I should not have taken it out on you."

'Correct. Just because you are not getting what you want does not mean you should be frustrated. You have the power to control your emotions.'

"I know, it's just..."

I wait for her to continue, though this lowered position I have for direct eye contact is not pleasant to maintain. If she thinks I am going to let her off easy on the subject, she does not understand the depths of my patience. Except, the tension now percolating between us is almost unbearable. Still, I know if I wait long enough, she will tell me what is on her mind. I am certain it will take some time for our bond to become comfortable, but Rayle needs to learn I am her closest ally and she can trust me.

It is something I quickly decided after spending even the barest amount of time with my pup's family. More often than not, her words are disregarded because of her endless energy and youth. Through our bond, I knew she was far more clever than many in her immediate family realized and gave credit. I sensed during the times others talked over her or cut her off that she just wanted someone to listen, despite the distracted, halting, or jumbled meaning of her words.

"My family has told me my whole life that I am not strong enough… or… or responsible enough to handle being a Stieti Tetsaa. Many of them even know what a trial it is to be bonded, and they still doubted. I proved them wrong. I am tall, strong, and my mind intact with you as my partner," Rayle says, finally.

I take a moment to understand what she actually meant. *'You want to prove to them you are capable by traveling to a war-torn realm doing what, exactly?'*

"When you put it like that, it makes little sense. Never mind."

'I am curious what your plan is with venturing to the Sun Realm.'

"It does not matter, Irigiim," Rayle says as her shoulders droop.

I push my nose against her–which spans more than the length of her body–leaving one side of her significantly more wet than the other. She giggles, but there is no joy in it. Despite her argument convincing me we should go to the other realm, I am still hesitant. She has not been in this world as long as I have and she has not seen the squabbles amongst the mages that pop up from time to time–though this war is by far the worse. I was a protector in my pack and the delta in me says stay away from all danger, but something changed when we bonded. My decisions cannot be so definitive anymore, nor can they be so fearful. Rayle has more complexities to her than what I was used to in my pack, and I dislike the emotional unbalance it causes to see my pup in such a dispirited state.

'We can go,' I say, doing my best to temper the reluctance from my tone. The last thing I want is to make her feel guilty for dreaming.

"What?"

My regal posture melts a little as I give into her hopes. I rest my snout on the ground to better smell the emotions of my bond partner. *'We can go to the other realm with two conditions.'*

Rayle jumps up and wraps as much of her arms around my large snout as best she can, which isn't much and has her dangling a little awkwardly from an air fold of my nose.

"Thank you, thank you–"

'You must agree to my conditions.'

"Anything."

She really is desperate.

'We must stay away from the main conflict of fighting, and you must have a purpose for going. I refuse to be a party to something that is merely to satisfy your curiosity,' I say.

"Of course! Can we go tonight? I want to see if all magicians are really as bad as the rumors say."

Her reason toes the borderline of curiosity, in my opinion, but I let it slide this time. I decide to consider it a legitimate argument in the pursuit of keeping the tribes safe. I have become soft in my bonding.

'Alright, we will look for a mage along the Eastern edge of the quarries tonight. Hopefully, it is sparsely populated. That is all I will concede to.'

Rayle grins at me, and so much joy seeps between us I want to stand and race around the palace gardens with wild abandon, but I restrain myself. There are too many witnesses to show such undignified behavior.

CHAPTER 6
CASTELL

The pale yellow moon surveilled Castell, full and seeming to cover the whole of the expanse of the north-east horizon. He, in return, gave his unwavering attention to the steady rise of the celestial disc. Stars clung to their spot in the sky despite the moon attempting to enthrall any who stepped outside. It was a grand sight, and it soothed some of the tension lining Castell's shoulders. Coming outside at night to watch the play of the heavens was the best part of living in the remote desert. Out here, on a cloudless night, nothing obscured a single star.

He lounged against the warm rock to counter the quickening chill and identified the constellations. The first one he spotted was Kikka Puthra. Whoever named the row of stars believed it to look like a line of flowers. To him, it seemed more like a splash of water against dry rock. The next to appear was Vaatla and his enemy, Lindu. The story of the two partners was a classic tale of enemies. Lindu, a vulture, liked to steal the kills from the hunter Vaatla, for he was the laziest of all his kin. Because of this, the hunter was always hungry. In anger, Vaatla forever chased Lindu across the sky. Sometimes he was successful in killing the wretched vulture, but Lindu always found a way back through the gates of death to torment the hunter once more.

Their story was an endless cycle of torment, one that he related to deeply. Not only did his thoughts on the war carry him in endless circles, but the repetitive task of chiseling away stones for minimal reward did as well. He needed to break the cycle or he too might one day have an endlessly repeating story among the stars. Definitely not the way he wanted to be remembered.

A rock skittered across the ground, breaking his concentration. Olke was pouncing on a mouse as it attempted to scamper toward its hole, the black-tip of her tail swishing happily from the successful hunt. Castell huffed a breathy laugh at his fox's antics. She always seemed to be a hungry thing. It didn't matter how much food he gave her. At least she could find her own meals. That was the one thing he was glad to not have trained out of her natural instincts.

Taking a fragment of the magic inside him, the symbol on his wrist glowed pale as he coaxed a breeze to pick up loose earth and create a small dust tunnel, blurring the stars. He watched his creation for a time before sending the swirl of air to roam across the desert and turned his attention back to the sky.

More stars dotted into existence and each new light Castell spotted became like a new idea coming to mind. He had accused his parents of cowardice for their pacifist ideas, but what his father said made sense. His mother was a talented Blood Mage and she would have likely been made to spread disease or suffocate the enemy. With her gift, she could just as easily heal someone as kill them, and the body, as resilient as it was, could also be deftly broken. Her gift could speed up or stave off death, and his mother–gods bless her–was one of the gentlest souls he knew. Whenever someone at the quarry suffered, Pleasa was often the first one to the injured's side, doing all she could to help. She had even been the one to convince his father to let him keep Olke. Knowing that, Castell could see how the life of a pacifist appealed to her, and it made him feel just the tiniest bit guilty for having such harsh thoughts toward the person who had taught him so much about love.

His father, though, was the greater riddle to him. Siggri had always been the stricter of his parents, and at least once a year would get in a heated exchange with another member at the Fire Talks. Ridiculously, it was often over the stories he told around the central fires, the members of the clan questioning the validity of his tales. As a Mind Mage, he could make people see whatever he wanted them to see, and it often ended in disputes because his memories and depictions differed from those in the community. He wasn't the only Indigo Mage in their small village, but he was certainly one of the most vocal. Which is what puzzled Castell the most. It made little sense that someone so engaging could convert to the life of a pacifist with ease. So, why was his father so adamant that he left because he would have been made to hurt people? He'd never gotten the impression that his father was unwilling to defend his beliefs.

Something out of the corner of his eye broke through his thoughts. A breeze kicked up as he glanced in the shadow's direction. The moon had risen high enough now that long inky shapes ran thick amongst the staggered rocks. His surroundings certainly lent to strange shapes, but there didn't seem to be anything that should have caught his attention. Still, there had definitely been a darker area that didn't seem to fit with the rest of the landscape. Olke, too, had studied the space to his left with some interest. Castell marked the shale hills for a few moments longer before shrugging and turning his eyes back to the sky.

The tumble of kicked rocks from the dwelling exit made him glance to see his father shuffling to his side. Castell sat up and dropped his eyes to the dust between his feet. Without invitation, his father dropped into a comfortable seat next to him. Castell conjured another miniature wind tunnel, this time around Olke, as a way to direct his unsettled energy. The small fox slowly started to rise through the gentle vortex, giving Castell something to fixate on to avoid his father's gaze.

"I love the constellations out here, they make for superb storytelling, but I miss our home and the stars of the forest," Siggri said.

Castell perked his ears, interested that his father would talk of such a subject.

"Son, I understand the conflict that flows in your veins. It was the same conflict that I had to resolve before your mother and I left our home and made a new life out here, but your conflict does not give you the right to be rude to your mother."

Castell curled inward. He'd already come to the conclusion and he did not like the correction from his father. Playing with his lip for a second, he opted for a gentler response. "What exactly was your conflict?"

"Before the war officially started, there were, of course, rumors of conflict about the two sides. I was very adamant that The Purists were correct in their assertions. Still am, just between you and me. I never openly said anything to my neighbors, but your mother knew my thoughts. The Clerics are as bad as the Sloe Horned Rattlers. They hide themselves behind impressive ideals, but produce nothing but poison."

Castell sat up, shocked. "So why did you not stay to fight!?"

"Because I cared more about your mother and you than I did about trying to prove who was right," Siggri answered casually, but conviction lay at the base of it.

Castell grabbed Olke as she floated almost out of the top of his wind tunnel, only for her to leap from his arms and run back to the base of it and rise again, eager to repeat their game. He tried to process what his father was saying, but the little fox was sketching such antics with the wind tunnels that he had to first snatch her mid-rise out of the twister and dissipate it while she struggled in his grasp before he could think enough to answer. When the words finally came out, they were acrid on his tongue. "Yet, you have told me my whole life that we should stay neutral to the conflict." He couldn't keep the accusatory tone from his voice.

"I was never seeking to mislead you, Castell." Siggri sighed. "The truth? The longer I have lived here, away from the battles, the more I have been convinced that both sides need to come to a compromise and stop this endless fighting. I may not agree with the things you said inside, and it will break my heart to see you go, but I will support you in your life." Reluctantly he added, "No matter where it takes you."

"You think I should join the fight?"

"No," came the decisive reply. "I do not want to possibly lose my firstborn to a senseless war! But your mother and I are not here to control you. That is not the gods' teachings."

Castell petted Olke, smoothing her fur from the black tips to the base of her ears. Finally, he said, "I see your and Ama's point of view, but I have to be involved somehow. Eventually, one side is going to win, and whether I choose the winning side... at least I have chosen. For me, pacifism is not the right choice."

"Son, I left because your mother is a gentle person and she wanted nothing to do with the fighting. My concern has always been for my family first, but I understand why you need to follow this road."

"Thanks, Papa."

Siggri grabbed his shoulder. He squeezed for just a moment as if he wanted to add something else, but let it be.

Castell nodded, everything his father said weighing heavily on his chest. "I will let you know after the next group of traders come through what I have decided."

"Time is always a friend when making big decisions. Goodnight, Son."

"Goodnight."

Castell didn't know what he was going to do, but he needed to decide soon. Leaving would undoubtedly break his mother's heart, as his father said, but it was reassuring to know she would still accept his decision. That his father would support his choice was comforting as well. He foresaw his brother spurning any thoughts he had, and his sister was unlikely to understand what all of this meant. However, Castell no longer felt torn about the lasting effects his decision would have on his family–just on himself.

Now the real question lay in whether he was ready to leave the only life he'd ever known behind, a life of safety and peace, only to venture into a world filled with violence and anger.

CHAPTER 7
IRIGIIM

'*What were you thinking, Rayle?!*'

I am foaming. If she were a Beast, we would currently be in a battle of teeth and claws. I am doing the only thing I can to keep myself level–I pace. My path leaves large swatches of an unrecognizable pattern of pads and claws on the loose earth. My pup cowers before me. She had no reason to before. Now, though, my massive size, a full eight meters above the top of her head, in addition to the ire teeming between our link, is making her tremble. A part of me is pained at causing her fear. I will never hurt her on purpose, but the feeling is easily dwarfed by my fury. She blatantly disobeyed the terms of our agreement, and I dislike being defied. It is my latent instinct from my time with the pack.

'*What was our agreement?*' I punctuate the question with a growl. '*Answer me!*'

'*You did not actually say that I could not approach one.*'

'*It should have been implied, Rayle. Especially with all of the precautions I was taking.*'

'The young man did not seem to be any harm. I was drawn to his contemplation,' she said. 'He was so still, staring at the moon, but there was this hum of restlessness about him. It is something I tend to recognize.'

'He could have been doing something as mundane as sketching lines in the dirt. He is still a danger by nature,' I say. She needs to understand the danger she almost put us in.

'But, Irigiim, he did not even try to attack when you pulled me from the Realm. Briefly, I saw him notice, and he did nothing.'

'Because he saw nothing! We were a mere shadow to him, and if he had seen us, he would have tried to attack us. Is that what you want? For us to be attacked? To feel pain?'

My pup scuffs her feet, sending up little puffs of dust. 'No... is that why you were so fearful? Because you did not want to be attacked?'

'I was fearful because magicians are dangerous. They seek out our kind. Make us slaves to their will. Turn us into shells of ourselves.'

'You do not know if the young man would have done that! I refuse to believe that all magicians are the same. Look at me and Serrett.'

I snap my teeth in frustration, making Rayle jump. I wish I could fight one of my old pack mates just to ease my muscles. Instead, I continue to pace. Perhaps the worst part is that, on top of my own seething emotions, every bit of her fear is echoing to me because of our infantile connection. I do not know how to make it stop, and it's inflaming my feelings. I quickly remind myself that I am not one of the lower beasts that only follow their base urges.

I am intelligent.

I am wise.

The pause eases the sharpness of my feelings and I take a deep breath before flopping to the dusty earth of the mesa, a cloud billowing around me. My pup doesn't deserve to feel this level of wrath from me. Anger, sure, but I'll reluctantly admit this is beyond what she deserves. We are partners. Even though I often view her as a pup, she is far from one and deserves my respect.

I settle with my legs crossed, semi-trapping Rayle so she cannot bolt. She would have to climb over my stacked paws, which would not be an easy feat, since one paw is taller than she is standing. I lower my head to encircle her protectively, but really it creates a lightless cave of fur. I'll probably have to move soon or she will become too hot.

'I am sorry, Rayle. I am upset by your lack of restraint, but I did not mean to act out in such a manner. Please forgive me.'

She stands for a few prolonged seconds still pressed against my leg, and I think she might be too frightened to move. Maybe she's surprised by my sudden change in attitude or my apology. Then I feel her turn to hug me. She's still trembling with the lingering fear in her system. I can tell by the ever so slight tugs where she's gripping my fur. Rayle isn't saying the words but her feelings are absolutely clear–she is sorry for pushing the bounds of prescribed limitations and for scaring me. It wasn't her intention to scare me.

At least I am forgiven for my outburst.

She's right, I never explicitly said she couldn't approach the magician we set out to observe, but that is because I thought she knew better. The truth is, I reacted out of fear. Magicians are vile creatures that do nothing but hurt themselves and others; I was terrified for myself and more so for Rayle. She is my chosen pup, my life. I lived so many years unattached, but the moment we created our bond at the ceremony, I knew it would be unbearable to lose her for any reason. And tonight, for the first time, I felt as though I almost had, and the overwhelming surge of fear and anger at the prospect had caught me off guard.

The silence sits too heavy between us, I need her to say something. I know she's forgiven me for the outburst, but the quiet is eating away at my tenuous composure.

'*Rayle, I am sorry I was afraid,*' I say, lifting my head to peer down at her and hopefully coax her into answering.

'*I know, Irigiim,*' she says, finally, and I can feel the depths of her forgiveness this time.

'*Then why do you remain so quiet?*'

'*Shock, I suppose.*'

'*You cannot be too shocked. You have been speaking to me mentally for the first time.*'

I feel pleasure in our link, but she goes for a barbed quip to ease the tension.

'*My jaw was trembling too much to form words...*'

After a moment I realize that there is a different stability between us that did not exist before; I always thought I would clearly recognize the moment our bond became as quotidian as breathing. I dislike that it came about this way, but the positive change in our relationship gives me hope.

'*You still have not answered me. If you are not shocked, why the silence?*'

'*I suppose... I do not understand your fear. When you pulled me back into the Shade Realm, an overwhelming amount of fear sparked your anger.*'

'*All magicians are wretched creatures.*'

'*That is not a singularly valid reason, Irigiim.*'

'*They are murderers,*' I reply.

'*I agree, but–*

'*I saw no point in either of us tempting fate to see if we would be harmed.*'

'*Fine, but I felt panic flood our link before you pulled me back into our realm,*' Rayle counters, pushing the issue.

Deep down I know I have no reason to be afraid now that she

and I are partners–but I still am. A bonded Beast cannot be pulled into the other realm to serve the magicians; in the moment of our bonding, we create a permanent tether tying us to this land. I know all of this, but the body does not always learn as quickly as the mind, and my instincts when it comes to threats are strong and difficult to redirect.

'*I did not want to lose you,*' I say. It's the truth as I have become incredibly attached, but it is not the whole truth.

Rayle is quiet for a moment and what she says next convicts me. '*I know you were thinking about your sire, Irigiim. You can trust me, you know?*'

I flatten my ears, ready to defend my actions, but then, like seeing light from the opening of the den for the first time, I notice a new level of harmony between us that once was nothing more than a vapor of an idea. The debacle that just happened with the magician was a lack of communication, but she's right, I can trust her.

Since we are bonded for life, I need her to know what happened in my past; why I sought to enter the bond. For the first time since the ceremony, I let my barriers crumble around Rayle.

She gasps as images flood her mind. Memories of the moment my sire was pulled from this realm are raw, and I do not honey-coat them. The forest that day had been pleasant. The smell of turned earth and sap filled my nose. Small game scattered from us, but we had recently eaten our fill. My sire and I were simply enjoying the stillness found only beneath the canopy of trees.

In the span of a breath, the world twisted, and I could feel his every frantic thought. Just like that, our connection was ripped from my teeth, shorn, leaving me utterly alone. My sire and I were close, and his horrified thoughts of knowing he was being pulled from the Shade to be caged beneath the Sun like a lower beast traumatized me. It was the worst fate any Beast imagined.

Becoming slaves to the magicians was not just about being pulled from our home, it was a desecration to us as intelligent creatures. The Sun Dwellers thought of us as powerful tools to be manipulated. It was degrading to say the least.

I whimper and rest my head across my leg as the memories wash me in a fresh flood of emotion. Rayle is on the ground, having fallen to all fours because the rush of memories made her weak, and I can feel her crying not just for me but with me. We stay like this for some time, sharing emotions back and forth across our link. My pup has never experienced a loss so grievous, so my memories distress her. I'm just thankful she does not judge me for what many of my kind perceive as weakness.

At some point, she makes her way back to me and does her best to snuggle as close as possible. Her comfort is a gift.

'Irigiim, I am so sorry for your loss. I understand why you reacted the way you did. You have my promise that I will never put myself in needless danger to satisfy my curiosity again,' she said. As if in a whisper she added, *'I would never want to cause you such pain on my behalf.'*

Her promise is a balm to my aching soul. I know I will lose her, eventually; it is the price to be paid with age, but at least I will not lose her unfairly to the hands of a mage.

CHAPTER 8
CASTELL

Castell set his last Sun Crystal in the basket. The day still had many hours left, and he could likely get a sixth crystal into his collection for the day, but he wanted to make it to the ale house in the lower settlement early to find a prime spot for listening in on the talk about the war.

Several villages occupied the mesa and those in the lowlands tended to be more involved in the conflict. As far as he knew, pacifism was exclusive to the few villages that lived up among the rocks, hermiting their homes inside the mined tunnels of the quarries.

After the talk with his father, Castell had made a promise to both his parents to seriously consider the choices before him and not take off simply because he felt restrained by his current life. It had been a hard promise to utter because he wanted to leave for that very reason, but his parents deserved a sound decision from him. His mother, especially, had been a selfless figure his entire life, and if a delay in his plans was what it took to honor her generosity, then he would gladly pay the fee.

A few weeks had passed since his outburst at dinner and another caravan of traders had finally made camp in their little corner of the world. Castell would not pass up this opportunity to hear news of the war firsthand. After the dinner and subsequent conversations with his father, he could no longer call his feelings about the war on the fence. He was definitely joining the fight, but he had yet to decide which side to support. In the past, he'd leaned toward the beliefs of the Purists. It was in that tradition his magic gift was nurtured, but that didn't mean the Clerics didn't have legitimate slants as well. Castell was fairly certain he would join the Purists when he left home, but he had promised absolute certainty of his decision, and for him, knowing which side to join was an integral part of that certainty.

Standing, Castell dusted the loose dirt from the tops of his legs. Honestly, he would be glad to leave behind the healthy layer of fine dust that covered him and everything else. How his mother kept their dwelling clean was a mystery. Castell had given up long ago on immaculacy. Chipping away at rock all day did not lend to any sort of cleanliness for any length of time.

Olke scampered out of the hole she had been using for an afternoon nap and perked her ears at his movement. She may not have known exactly what he was doing, but she was smart enough to know that he was leaving sooner than normal.

"Come, Olke. Let's go turn in my haul for the day and then clean up some before we go to the village. I'll give you a couple of eggs before we leave. How's that sound?"

She gave a chittering yip before waiting to see what he would do. Castell did not know if Olke could understand him, but she always seemed to have a canny way of being at the right place at the right time. His heart dipped a little as he watched the little creature. He could not take Olke with him when he left. It was far too dangerous and Castell cared too much about his companion to expose her to the threats of war. Taking her would be like taking his little sister to stand on the front lines.

Lifting the basket, he balanced it on his head before making his way to the quarry leader. The gruff man would not be happy he was leaving early, but nothing would stop him from making it to the ale house tonight.

CASTELL COUGHED, waving away the smoke filling the cramped room. It appeared he'd arrived at the perfect time. Most of the tables were brimming with patrons, each fisting a tankard of ale while picking at plates of chicken, bread, cheese, and vegetables. Lively chatter teemed as everyone waited for the traders to take the seats of honor on what normally was the musician's stage and spin their tales of the latest news. The leaders of the caravan, already in town, could likely hear every bit of the commotion from their rooms upstairs. He absently wondered if they dreaded making an appearance or if it gave them a thrill of pleasure to have so much attention centered on them. Probably the latter. He imagined it would be difficult to be in a customs trade and not like people.

Twisting and turning through the tables, Castell made his way to the bar. It'd been an hour trek down the hills to get here and he was plenty thirsty and ravenously hungry. The chicken plate he'd seen hadn't piqued his interest. Instead, he chose the other offering of meat pie and a pint to wash it down before pushing through the patrons to snag one of the few available spots.

Olke twisted in his satchel, her curiosity making her brave, and he saw the tip of her little black nose poke out the side. She could probably smell the beef in his dinner. Castell rested a hand on the bag to still Olke and pulled apart his dinner to sneak her a few pieces of meat. Hopefully that would keep her from feeling adventurous. Castell didn't want to get booted from the establishment without hearing the news.

A keen hush settled over the room as someone noticed the traders' appearance, a blanket snuffing the fires of conversation. Reverent greetings were given to the men as they made their way to the front of the room. It was amazing how two men could garner such respect simply because they traveled and sold things for a living. The bar maid gave them each a drink, and it was a silent room that watched as each man lit his pipe. Castell was glad they were on the musicians' platform. Even from his congested space in the back he could easily see the traders.

"Gents, you honor us with your presence. No sense in beating around the bush as we all know what information you want," the first merchant said, his voice canorous.

He was a dark-haired man with pale eyes. Castell had never seen snow, but the man's eyes were exactly the color he had imagined when hearing his father's description of the cold flakes. The second merchant was a stark contrast to his partner. His pale hair looked even more bleached from their short stint traveling through the desert and he had dark eyes that absorbed every speck of brightness around him. Both were dressed in pants and loose tunics with sleeveless duster coats. Their too-warm clothes looked stifling to Castell and set them apart from the locals.

"The war has grown worse, friends."

The listeners inhaled collectively, a chorus of horrified breaths. Castell had also sucked in a breath. Worse? What did that mean? Was one side finally giving up the fight? Was it too late for him to join?

"The Clerics have gained strength in the last year, calling more and more Shade Demons to their aid. The rumors say the

Purists also know how to chain such horrid Beasts, but they refuse to use such appalling creatures for their gain. It has not helped their cause."

The second merchant added, "Many have lost hope in the Purists' ability to protect the ancestral way of life."

Murmurs circulated as everyone digested the information. Castell didn't know any of the surrounding people, so he contemplated the information silently. It was time for him to join the fight, and he would do it at the side of the Purists. He didn't really know what Shade Demons were, stories painted them as abominations, and anyone that summoned them willingly did not deserve his support. With a detached sigh, he released the last vestiges of his pacifist ideology. The world was definitely changing, and he needed–wanted to change with it.

CHAPTER 9
TRIGIIM

'I do not enjoy stepping around this collection of humans, Rayle,' I say with more irritation than necessary. I am consciously working on improving my instinctive reactions to situations, never wanting another incident like the quarries. *'It is time we leave and return to the assigned posting.'*

The streets at the Oasis are plenty wide to accommodate Beast, but humans will easily occupy a space if the space allows for it. Why do humans feel the need to spread out and occupy the entirety of a space? I must be careful not to step on them, which irritates me, though most do their best to get out of my way. I wish humans were more like animals and respected each other's territory. Instead, they jostle and skim past one another in a complicated dance. The worst part is the constant brushing against my paws because of near misses from too little space or distracted shoppers. What makes it even more difficult to maneuver are all the awnings jutting out from the fronts of the low, sprawling buildings. My height above everything makes it so that many of these brightly tinted shade cloths in their solids and stripes block my view, making it impossible for me to navigate easily. If it wouldn't crush the buildings, walking on top of them would save me a great deal of trouble.

The crowds are ruffling me, plus I am hot. I am a wolf of the forest, I prefer the cool wet air beneath the large deciduous trees of my home instead of this dry arid heat that parches my throat. Longing fills me.

Now if I can only convince my pup. A tiny part of me is also reluctant to leave because this exploration of the Isokanii capital is important to my pup. I will always do my best to accommodate Rayle. I didn't have to join her on this arduous trek through the market streets. I could have easily stayed in one of the many constructed dens at the palace, but at the time I wasn't in the mood to spend an afternoon alone. Now, though, I want nothing more than cool water and a nap.

'I told you, Irigiim, go back to the palace if you do not wish to be here. There is much more to see!'

Rayle practically crows the last part, I groan. I do not want to see more awnings and crowds.

'What, exactly, is the point of this shopping again?'

The idea is completely foreign to me since we Beast simply take what we want, or, most commonly, here at the Oasis, are given whatever we want out of reverence for our kind. When my pup told me shopping is bartering baubles for other useless items, I balked. So far I have witnessed her trade beads, cheap weapons, and small vials of liquid to merchants for clothing, bracelets, and more beads.

The exchange of beads puzzles me more than any of her other purchases. Rayle explained that she was giving the merchants wooden beads to receive glass beads in return. She likes to put them amongst the long braids of her hair as decoration. This makes even less sense. Glass beads are heavier than wooden beads, so why use them? She shrugged at my line of questioning and ignored me. I concluded that if she believes it will not hinder her abilities–like standing or fighting–then I will not cavil at her decision. The only positive thing I see in all this exchange of materials is that my pups' obsession with frivolous decorations in her hair allows me to always know where she is located. Rayle can be stealthy, sure, but with my sensitive hearing, she will never actually sneak up on me.

'It is fun, Irigiim. To exchange conversations with others to get the things you need. It is like the markets at home but on a much grander scale! I love it!' Rayle says.

The shopping still seems unnecessarily frivolous. However, it is the one thing she has in common with her sister. Everything else with Serrett, I noticed, is open for debate or a fight. I am actually surprised my pup's older sister did not join us on the excursion today. It has been two weeks since the wedding ceremony, so she is not as confined as the week previous. Although, now that I ponder it, Rayle mentioned that Serrett is to leave soon for some extended journey with her new mate. It is possible she is busy with preparations.

'Rayle, everything aside, we need to return to our territory,' I say, bringing up the one thing I know will dampen her mood.

Which it does. Instantly.

There is so much hesitation coming across our link, it even makes me feel strange. Finally, she says, *'I agree that I have drawn this out for far longer than necessary.'*

Her frankness surprises me. Can my pup be maturing?

'I only ask that you let me draw it out a little further.'

My hope of a more seasoned Rayle vanishes like water on this hot day.

'In what way will you delay us now?' I sigh.

More hesitation, and I imagine my pup biting her lip as she tries to sort her words into a viable argument.

'I would like to travel to the Southern coast before returning to our home.'

'Why? The sea is the same near our home as it is in the south. What do you hope to learn?'

'It is not about learning anything, Irigiim,' Rayle says, more than a little frustrated with my lack of understanding.

'Then what is the point?'

'Not everything has to be about learning something.'

'I do not understand. I take in smells which tell me where food is located or I hear noises that might present danger, all of which help me learn the things I need to know to survive.'

Rayle is quiet for so long I think she has blocked our connection in an attempt to ignore me. If that is the case, I will leave her, since we have apparently come to an impasse. I am actually surprised when she speaks.

'Irigiim, we have not been connected for long, but there is something that you need to know about me. I know I am exuberant, something you could not have determined during the ceremony, so I will tell you this directly. I find peace in nature, the things the gods have created, just like I find peace when I am practicing my blades. Stillness, if you will. That is why I want to go south. It is a place I have not seen, and it is a place that I want to store into my memory to cherish. That is what I mean when I say it is not always about learning something.'

Rayle's words are impassioned and strong. She has not thundered them through my mind, but there is genuine feeling behind each word. I mull over what she said, and come to only one conclusion. Water is still water, whether it is from the East or the South. It is a terribly human sentiment to want to see a landscape from a different direction.

I like my forest, the quiet, the shade, the tall trees for me to roam under, and I am content to stay there; except for my decision to bond, I never left my home. Why would anyone want to explore the constant changes of a loose shifting earth or the sway of tall grasses, when there is the speckled light upon a forest floor or the smell of moss in the morning?

As much as I do not want to, I give into her request. I hope bonding isn't turning me soft.

I do not want to be here or anywhere else, but I comfort myself knowing we will return home soon enough. I've spent hundreds of years in my beloved forest, so I can give up a few more weeks in these intolerable surroundings to give Rayle a chance to glimpse something she's never seen. I may not understand it, but I gave up my personal rights when I agreed to the bond. My pup and I are partners. She went through an incredible amount of pain for me to bond with her, so a few more weeks of doing something other than what I prefer is bearable–for now. If she asks me again to go to another place, I am going to dig in my paws.

When I tell her of my consent, she isn't as overjoyed as the first time I agreed to her request, but I feel contentment between our link. Almost as if she understands why I am reluctant to give my agreements. It makes me consider that I may not be giving Rayle enough credit. I already know she is smart, but maybe she knows me better than I think she does.

CHAPTER 10
CASTELL

A rock skittered down the road after coming in contact with Castell's sandal. Olke yipped and chased it, perking her ears in his direction once she conquered the small object.

She is so proud. Castell smiled at his pet.

Despite his attempt to leave her behind for safety, Olke had easily escaped her keeper, his little sister, and came after him. He had camped for the night away from the road in the shelter of an outcropping, and when he woke in the morning, she was curled next to him like every night since he'd found her. At that point, he was too far into his journey to take her back, and clearly she would not accept being left behind, so Castell cradled her in his arms and continued on. Doubts about his decision to leave home traveled in his mind like the smoke circling the campfire the night before, but Olke's loyalty had heartened him to carry on with his resolve to join the war.

His mother had not been happy about his intent to leave. Neither was his father, but he at least accepted it with composure.

His mother, on the other hand, let sober tears stain her cheeks, mutely guilting Castell to change his mind. Instead, he'd stood there as if someone had cut his tongue from his mouth; neither comforting his mother nor defending his position. He couldn't very well tell her it was going to be okay, he was joining a war, and she would never agree with his decision, so silence seemed like the best option. If he had been leaving to explore new settlements or make his way in the world they would have rejoiced, but he was leaving to join The Purists. He loved his parents and his siblings, but Castell refused to let his allotment in life be mining a small corner of a dusty quarry.

Tiecia, his sister, had taken his announcement as expected. She joined his mother in her tears, but hers came out more as tragic sobs. But he suspected her tears were simply because he was leaving. It made sense, being only eight. Tiecia had been a serendipitous addition to their family and Castell loved his little sister fiercely, but the age difference between them had always made him feel more like a parent than a sibling to her. She was sheltered from conversations about the war, so while she understood why he was leaving, in her mind he was just leaving, and that was all the reason she needed to be sad.

His brother, Averek, had not been so docile. Castell endured at least an hour's worth of a diatribe about how he was abandoning the family and not concerning himself with ancestral obligations. Castell had lost count of how many times his brother had called him selfish. Sadly, his brother had little to stand upon because Castell was beholden to no one. Sure, he'd spent many nights eating the final meal of the day with his parents and little sister, but he also had a space of his own and was completely independent. Castell contributed very little in the grand scheme of things when it came to mining, so what was the point of staying? Now, with the emptying from his set of rooms, someone who truly desired a quiet life could settle in Sun Glimmer.

Averek's anger was more likely because he feared losing his older brother, though he'd never admit it. The summers between them were few, and the closeness they shared made the sting of his leaving all the worse. Castell understood why his brother could not understand his position. While he'd spent his years in the quarries of Sun Glimmer dreaming of other places and other work, Averek had easily found contentment in marrying and mining Sun Crystals for a decent profit as an Amber mage. His younger brother had never understood why Castell didn't take a wife. Sure, there were plenty of young women in the greater area that he probably could have been happy with, but Castell had deep down always known he wouldn't be content tending ground he didn't want.

His brother's anger had been so immense that he wouldn't speak to Castell no matter how many times he'd visited the small network of caverns that were his brother's home. He had even delayed his leaving by several days just so he could tell his brother goodbye. Finally, he'd decided that waiting would not bring Averek to say goodbye. But on the morning of his departure, Averek stood in the cool mist with his parents and little sister to say farewell. It was to his little brother that Castell gave the longest hug.

Now, two weeks' worth of walking and bartering rides every so often had gotten Castell to Whispering Flats, a large city near the Whispering River. Amazingly, with all the fighting this city had seen, trees still rooted along the bank and buildings still stood, but it was a far cry from the forest home his father had shown him in illusions. Lush grass had given way to dusty ground and leafless bushes. The decimation from battles along with the need for space and strong thick wood for construction had taken its toll on the once lush area. Now it looked desperate. Castell wished a conjured storm would wipe away the years of war that had marked this city, except that would only hurt more than help, and this city had seen enough damage. Whispering Flats was one of the last major cities to endure the brunt of the fighting since the start of the war, and from what others told him along the road, it was the Purists' headquarters.

With a sigh and determined step, Castell embraced the thought that this city could be the end of his days, fitting since he'd started them here as a baby. He didn't know where to go in order to join The Purists. For now he needed to find food and a place to sleep.

The last specks of light tinged the horizon. The principal thoroughfare was dark, making it difficult to locate a place to rest. The use of magic so opposite from his own would tire him, but desperate to see, Castell let a cloud-shaped illumination form in his palm bright enough to shed light on the signs above doors. He traversed the main road, looking for an inn still in business. A noisy building drew his attention and he found an inn and tavern with light spilling out of the windows. Castell squinted at the sign. It looked like someone had carved a river oyster into the wood.

Picking up Olke, he set her in his pack and closed the flap. She squirmed inside the confinement, likely putting claw marks into his clothes. "Stop that, Olke," he admonished. "Unless you want to sleep by yourself outside tonight, stop squirming."

She settled, turning into nothing more than extra weight in his satchel. Satisfied, Castell pushed his way into the building. Lively music clung to the rough wooden walls, but one look at the patrons told him that the years of the war had levied the people into hopelessness. Smiles existed, sure, but they were halfhearted, and there was no mistaking the haunted look in each eye.

Hunched shoulders and the solace found at the bottom of an ale mug seemed to be the only concerns in the room. Silently, Castell commended the residents of Whispering Flats for having resiliency amidst constant distress. They never knew when the Clerics would attack, and from what he saw, the people here rebuilt and pushed forward no matter what.

A powerful scent caught his attention as the lid of a large iron pot was removed. The tavern maid used a ladle to scoop out what looked to be a sad stew, but the smell still enticed him. Anything would do after surviving on bread, dried meats, and hard cheeses during his travels. Whatever herbs and spices they used, it was working because his mouth watered at the idea of a hot meal. As soon as he secured a room, he would come down for a bowl.

"Excuse me, sir, do you have any rooms?" Castell asked, after sidling up to the bar.

The wafer thin bartender turned toward him. Dark bands decorated the man's eyes, and Castell instantly felt sorry for him. The poor man probably just wanted well-fitting clothes and to run his tavern without trepidation of it being destroyed on a daily basis.

"Sure thing, son. I got one room left and it'll be five silvers," the keeper said.

Castell handed several pieces of his saved gold to the man. The keeper's eyes rounded, but he kept his mouth shut.

"I might be here a while. Hopefully that will cover me?"

Suddenly, the keeper looked nervous. "It's not much of a room, lad."

"It's alright. I'll take whatever you have." Castell smiled in an effort to ease the man's worries.

"As you wish," the man said, handing over an iron key.

After climbing the stairs to examine the room, a part of Castell wished he'd never made such a conciliatory statement. The space could squeeze in two single beds if a magician were powerful enough just to cast the furniture into existence, which is probably what happened here, since he could barely take three steps without running into something. Still, the bed was softer than the ground; the quilt looked warm enough, and it was a far cry from sleeping out in the open under stars with curious creatures and insects for company.

Shutting the door, Castell set his pack on the floor, allowing Olke to hop out. Immediately, she went about sniffing the corners of the room. He would have to leave her here while he returned to the main room for a bowl of the stew and some bread. Maybe in the meantime she would find a mouse to be her dinner.

Standing, Castell smiled. Though his surroundings were grim, he'd made it to his destination. His life now felt like there was something tangible to it–a sense of purpose. To get his destiny started, all he needed was to find someone to talk to him about the war, and where he could find The Purists. He hoped he wouldn't start any tavern fights with his questions.

CHAPTER II
IRIGIIM

"See, Irigiim, the water is beautiful, yes?" Rayle asked.

'I told you of my opinion on the way here, and it has not changed,' I reply.

My pup sighs with just an edge of frustration seeping between our links. I have tried to put myself in her shoes, but the experiment proved to be rather foundering.

Glancing behind me I say, *'I do appreciate the soon-to-be harvested fields, though. The sound of the wheat is systematic and comforting. It is a reminder of the boughs of the forest as they sway in the wind.'*

Rayle turns to take in that view as well, but I can feel it is not the same for her. Sure, it is pretty, but something about the ocean calls to her. My pup moves to the cliff edge to dangle her bare feet and absorb the view.

I too settle into a comfortable position to watch the day slip into a more quiet night. The moon is not on display, but the obsidian sky allows the stars to take the attention and they certainly revel in it. The Isokanii would say Kiiholee is shy and ashamed of the reflection he sees from his sister Ostiimii. Despite Jurana's love for him, he turns his face from the world to grieve. It is only with his sister's coaxing that he will again turn to reveal himself before concealing his face once more. Rayle tells me the stars are the sparkle of Jurana's tears since the first gods did not love her brother. I appreciate the imagination of humans, but I truly cannot bring myself to believe in their deities. My favorite celestial body is an argent chalky portion of the sky stretching North to South. It is like all the stars gather in one place and there are so many it creates a bleached spot that wants to rival the moon. I do not know why I like this portion of the sky so much. I just do.

I turn my gaze toward the vast ocean as the last rays of light dip below the horizon. The wind blows the salty air, giving it an extra sting inside my nose. I sneeze in a useless attempt to remove the sensation. The winds are not as harsh along the edges of my forest home, perhaps because they are to the West instead of the South, or maybe it is because of the tall trees that protect the coastline. Whatever the reason, I definitely prefer there to here. The rough waters feel out of balance to me, but I cannot quite put my paw on why I am so bothered by the commotion. The Isokanii would say that Giiha is purposely agitating his sister Ostiimii.

Not long after we were bonded, my pup asked me what the beliefs of Beast were, and I could not give her an answer. It is simply not something Beast discuss. I told her I knew deep in my core something or someone created me. The information I withheld was that I did not believe it was the gods of the Isokanii. Since our bond, everything I have heard from the humans only convinces me their stories are written as a way for them to explain the world. I have never sensed my thoughts upsetting my pup, but I see fit not to speak of them again–as a safety measure. It seems impractical to me to rationalize something like the moon or waves of the ocean when there is a straightforward answer. Rayle, however, has been praying to Jurana for years, long before bonding to me, and I am not about to upset the balance of something for the sport of toying with it. That was only something I did as a puppy, and it was trained out of me by my dame.

Once the horizon gives way to full night, I rise and stretch, letting my nails dig into the rocky earth. I assumed Rayle would be ready to leave now that the sun had set, but when she does not move, I open the link between us to explore what she is thinking. I am taken aback by her emotions. Just as she had said, a sense of tranquility and peace is there that had not existed, yet there is an underlying tension. A protective instinct comes over me, and I want to take her burdens and solve every single one of them. *'Rayle, you can talk to me. We may not always agree, but I am your bond partner, and as such, I can be trusted,'* I say.

The words float in the space between our mental link, imploring me to take them back, but I have no reason to believe my words upset her. However, they do the opposite of comfort and make her more anxious.

'Irigiim, walk the beach with me.'

The request confuses me, and I nearly refuse because I dislike sand between the pads of my feet. The grittiness irritates me, but how can I refuse my pup? There is definitely more she wants to say, the feeling of it dangling between us like her feet over the cliff edge.

I lower myself so Rayle can sit between my shoulders. Once she grips my fur, I back up just enough to give myself a running leap. I am large, of course, but even for me, the jump down to the water is a distance. Bunching my back muscles, I propel myself forward. As my front paws push from the edge, I use my strengthened back legs to propel myself away from the cliff face, landing with a heavy bone-rattling thud onto my front paws, and a spray of black sand and water. I close my eyes and mouth at the last minute, and it is a good thing I do, otherwise I would have had the awful gritty feeling in places I do not want it. My pup was smart enough to clamp her mouth together so she did not accidentally bite her tongue.

I trot in a circle to let my exhilarated heart slow to a normal rhythm. Thrilled that I made such a clean jump, I howl my pleasure. The cliff face is no match for my agility. My antics produce a smile from Rayle.

Once my pup is no longer on my back, I give a hearty shake to remove the bits of sand that managed to cling to my fur. I absolutely do not understand why anyone likes this stuff.

'Aw, Irigiim, you just got me dirty,' Rayle complains.

'My apologies.'

Though I feel no remorse since I do not like sand. My feelings must have leaked through the link because my pup calls me out on it. She must not have been too vexed because Rayle only pats me on the paw before making her way down the beach. I wait, pointing my nose in different directions, taking in all the scents, before following her at a very sedate pace. My strides are enormous compared to any humans, so I can easily overtake her if needed. The wind, now that I am perpendicular to it, is not as bothersome, but something is still distorted. I try to ignore it since I cannot come to any logical conclusion for my unease, but that does not stop my ears flicking and my nose twitching.

'You asked me what was bothering me, and the truth is that I am afraid to return home. It is why I have been delaying with these extra ventures,' Rayle confessed.

'Why do you not wish to return home?'

'I miss the forest same as you, and do not bother denying it, your feelings have been quite clear.' I cringe at being caught by my

unspoken words. I really need to learn how to better block my feelings.

'I am avoiding home because of my family.'

'Your family loves you, Rayle.'

'Of course they do, but I also do not fit into their mold. I am too reckless, too emotional, too indecisive–I am just too much of anything and everything. These few weeks have been freeing for me. Not having someone constantly telling me what I'm doing wrong, or not as expected.'

This conversation is nothing new, but I definitely do not blame her for bringing it up again. Since learning the language of the Isokanii, I have come to understand that words are spoken in two ways. Some are like the edge of a sharp rock. They cut deep and hurt, but eventually they will heal with minimal damage; or they are like the rock that wind has marred into an uneven edge. Those dig deep and leave a lasting memory far more painful because they never really heal. I have experienced both.

'*I understand,*' I say, and I share the memories of a few times with my sire where his thoughts toward me were less than generous.

I miss my sire. His violent end will forever haunt me, but that does not change the damage he wrought with his opinions on the world. It is why I still question my decision to be bonded from time to time. That is one thing I keep buried like a winter's store of bones. I never want Rayle to doubt my loyalty to her just because I have some lingering doubts from the shadow of my sire's opinions.

'*It still surprises me how similar the Beast and Isokanii are to each other,*' Rayle says.

It is not something that occurred to me until I was bonded, but my pup is correct. '*I think lack of understanding is a fault in intelligent, sentient creatures as a whole.*'

Rayle agrees, and then asks, *'Can you see any place to shelter for the night? I am suddenly very exhausted.'*

I look around, but it is with the help of my nose that I find us a place to rest. Nestled between the tall cliff and a rock outcropping, there is a spot large enough to mostly shelter us from the wind. I find it because the place holds a smell of dampness that does not otherwise linger on the beach due to the steady winds. The added moisture will keep me cool, while my body heat will keep Rayle warm.

'Over here, and we can stay one more day to bolster your spirits,' I say.

'Thank you, Irigiim.'

'However, we should return after. Avoiding your family will not make the problem cease to exist.'

Rayle sighs. It's such a heavy thing, too. *'I know, but I thank you for your solace, nonetheless.'*

I give her a light nudge as she inches her way into the depths of my fur.

'If we are going to be here another day, we should not waste it. This seems to be a rather quiet part of the beach and we should practice our coming together,' I add, finding a comfortable spot for my head.

While yawning, Rayle agrees.

For the first time, I am truly appreciating the bond between us. It is more special than any relationship I had with my sire, and it is something I treasure increasingly each day. I will fight tooth and claw before releasing it from my grasp.

CHAPTER 12
CASTELL

Castell found himself crammed between groups of men with eyes already well glazed from ale consumption, and he wondered if the ales were that much stronger here because fighters needed to forget the horrors of war, or they just had more of it. Fermented drink of any kind was rare and exceedingly expensive in Sun Glimmer since any water that sluiced through the porous rocks was used for basic needs. Purified water needed to make any sort of ale was used solely for hydration or storage for the crops during the dry season. Blood Magicians could purify water because of their ability to detect microbes, something his mother had told him, but it certainly wasn't a priority in their remote hamlet. Some of the older widowed residents ventured into making fermented drinks, but only as a hobby with their own water supply.

Taking a tentative bite of his food, Castell had to fight a gag from escaping at the overtly bland meal, a huge disappointment from what he smelled when first walking in the door. The meat and vegetables had been stewed for so long that all the flavors boiled out, which he didn't think possible. Apparently, he was disillusioned from eating dry rations for so long. He took a gulp of ale just to have a flavor in his mouth.

How can anyone eat this stuff?

"Bad, yeah?" A man across the table and a few seats over asked.

Castell grimaced. "Yeah."

"Don't worry, Orttwin knows it's no good."

"Who is Orttwin?"

The man nodded his head in the keeper's direction. "He's the owner, lad. Orttwin does the best he can, given the circumstances."

"I can only imagine," Castell replied, looking down at the pathetic stew. It certainly wasn't what he was used to at home. One bite of this and he was already dreaming of his mother's cooking. He couldn't complain–wouldn't–because coming here was his choice. His mother's cooking was now far out of reach. He tried to think positively. At least this was better than dried road rations. Maybe.

"What's your name, lad?"

"Castell."

"Brion," the man replied, extending a hand. "Where you from?"

"Sun Glimmer, you have probably never heard of it. Small settlement in the Northeast corner of the quarries."

"Can't say that I have," Brion said, sliding over to be a little more in front of him. "What brought you to Whispering Flats? You're young, but I can tell you're well past any normal age for leaving home."

Castell wondered how forthcoming he should be with Brion. Would he laugh and think him foolish? Yet, this might be the opening he needed to learn where to sign up for service.

"Honestly? I came to learn more about the war. We are pretty isolated in Sun Glimmer."

Brion narrowed his eyes. "Decided peace and quiet wasn't exciting enough, so you came to seek fame and glory?"

"Hardly."

Brion gave a derisive snort. "Why else would a lad like you come? This is no place to build a life."

Looking him in the eye, Castell said, "Because it discontented me living as a pacifist. I do not agree with the fighting. War does not actually solve the problem, but staying out of it would not resolve things faster, either. I am not naïve enough to think that I will turn the tide of war, but I still wanted to help."

Brion gave him a thoughtful look, and with a purse of his lips, nodded.

"So, what side have you chosen?"

"I have not yet," Castell lied. He didn't want to make an enemy of someone he just met, at least not until he'd had some additional information. "Though, I have a preference toward one side more than the other."

"And which side is that?"

"Why should I tell you? If we are in disagreement, then it could spell the end of my journey. I want to fight in the war, but I do not have a death wish."

Brion stared at him for the briefest of seconds before he burst out laughing. "Giilo, Arlon, Liion! Scoot over here and meet this lad. I like you, kid."

The three men Brion called grumbled at having to shift out of their tired hunches, but nevertheless made their way to the summons. It took an excessive amount of disgruntled murmurs from other patrons as they were forced to move aside for the three men to sit next to him and Brion. When the commotion settled,

Giilo occupied Castell's left, Arlon his right, and Liion sat across the table next to Brion.

"Alright, Brion, what's the hubbub all about?" Arlon asked.

"The lad here wants to fight, but he doesn't know which side to choose. I say we need to recruit him to our side."

"What side would that be?" Castell jumped in before they could begin their diatribes.

"This is a Purists tavern, boy," Liion said, with a rough growl that didn't match his lanky form.

Castell nodded. "I still would like to hear your thoughts on the two factions."

"Hoho! We got ourselves a thinker," Giilo teased, giving his shoulder a light shove.

"All you need to know is that The Clerics are wrong," Liion commented, yet there was definitely an underlying threat that if Castell didn't believe him, then the worst could be expected. At least Liion was on the other side of the table and should he decide to act on the subtle threat, the most he could do was kick him in the shins.

Castell raised his hands to edge away from an argument. "I never said I did not agree with you, but what is the point of a fight if you do not know why you are fighting?"

Arlon raised his mug. "The kid makes a good argument, Liion. You've been in this fight since the beginning. Do you even remember why?"

"Of course I remember why! I do it for my children and grandchildren! No one, and I mean no one, should be oppressed by others who think they know what's best"—Liion stood to lean across the table and stare Arlon in the eyes—"and being told where you rank on a societal scale is not freedom, it's slavery!"

A round of cheers from the closest patrons to their group floated above the crackle of fire and noise of conversation.

"Ho, Liion, we're on the same side!" Arlon said, as he leaned away from the confrontation.

"Don't ask me any more stupid questions, and I'll not be so angry."

Castell's eyes grew at the extreme rebuttal. *This is what's wrong with the war. Others are not willing to listen and compromise.*

"Just ignore Liion's intensity," Brion said. "He's had it harder than others."

"Maybe if you all had a little *more* intensity, we wouldn't be losing so many battles," Liion grumbled.

"Now that's not fair," Giilo piped in, "we're all doing the best we can."

"So, what side are you backing, kid?" Arlon asked.

Castell scanned the faces of the men. "Well, my question still has not been answered."

The four men grumbled and sighed.

Brion was the one that finally answered. "The Clerics believe that those with more power should rule over those that are weaker."

"I know that, but what makes their system broken? The Clerics want to set up a schooling system for those that want to learn, yes?" Castell asked.

Giilo snorted.

"Not really, lad," Brion answered. "They want the schools to teach people, yes, but it's so they can be controlled later. I was a fighter for the Clerics, and it's nothing but back-stabbing and doing whatever it takes to get ahead. They pit the different magics against one another to find the strongest. Only those in power are valued, and that's not a system anyone should be part of. We're better off appreciating each individual's unique abilities."

Castell nodded his head. Having schools was, in theory, a good idea; he wouldn't know nearly as much about his Weather skills if it wasn't for someone wiser. His parents had said that's how communities used to function long before the rise of the schools. People took care of one another. For whatever reason, someone thought that method of teaching wasn't adequate.

Still, there was a part of him that liked the idea of having a place of learning. He was the only one in his family with Weather Magic, and growing up he relied on the others in Sun Glimmer that had his same gift. It benefited him, but what if there had been no one at all? The odds of that were extremely low considering only six variants of magic existed, but at home there had been only a handful of Weather Mages out of the fifty people that lived and mined the quarries. Perhaps, once the war was over, there could be talks of schooling that was actually fair to all.

"I think there is some value in having a schooling system that is open and fair to those that want to learn—"

"You have got to be joking with me," Liion said.

Castell narrowed his eyes at the man. "*However*, I agree it should not be a system founded on control and the encouragement of power. So... how do I go about joining the Purists?"

Brion smirked, almost as if he knew from the beginning Castell's answer. "Today is your lucky day, kid, I'm one of the commanders. What's your gift?"

"Weather."

Arlon whistled. "Nice. We don't get many of you since most feel their gift is ineffective for fighting."

Castell groaned. "Please, I beg you, do not make me work with Nature, I have watered enough fields."

"Depends, lad. Food is always needed. How strong are you?" Brion asked.

"I am not sure how to answer that, but I used to maintain light breezes all day long while working the quarries on nothing more than three cups of water."

Liion grunted, albeit reluctantly. "Impressive, kid."

Brion smiled. "Can you actually create and control weather patterns and not just use what's already in the atmosphere?"

"Yes."

"Then I think we definitely have a place for you on the front lines."

Castell gulped and nodded. It was a good thing his mother was not here, otherwise she'd break down at his suddenly being thrust into war. She was such a cautious person, always making sure that she had all the information before taking action. He was doing the exact opposite. He shook his head to fling away the image of his mother's sad face.

"It's been quiet the last couple of days," Arlon said, "you think they're preparing another attack soon?"

"Just assume they're always preparing an attack," Giilo said before taking a swig of his ale.

"Meet me at the command tent on the East edge of town tomorrow morning before noon, lad, we'll get you squared away," Brion said.

"Yes, sir. Well, thank you for talking with me, but it has been a long day of walking, and I am going to sleep."

Giilo gave him a mischievous grin, "Don't let the Demons get ya."

"We're not trying to scare the kid away!" Arlo punched his friend in the arm.

"He's gonna have to learn, eventually!"

Castell shook his head and left the main room. There had been plenty of rumors in each of the villages and towns he'd gone through about large obsidian-colored creatures with a taste for death, and they sounded terrifying. He hoped he didn't have to come face to face with one.

CHAPTER 13

TRIGIIM

'*We must try again,*' I insist.

The sooner we leave this beach and return home, the better. Today the waters are even more choppy and the winds more cruel. The sea is sending me a message but I do not have the language to decipher it. The best word I know to describe what is happening to the water is diseased. One of the earliest lessons I learned as a pup is to stay away from things that have a rotten smell, and right now I am surrounded by it, making my stomach curl. Maybe everything feels discordant because we are not in a familiar area, and I just desperately want to be home in the stillness of the forest. I do my best to ignore what feels like augural signs and keep focused on the task at hand, which is my pup putting valiant effort into not joining with me.

Rayle scrunches her face and sinks into the sand, on the verge of crying out her complaints. My pup knows I am right because being able to join as one is an important aspect of a Stieti Tetsaa, but so far our joining has been an unpleasant process for her. On some level, I understand her hesitation because of our connection, but it is not as physically painful for me as it is for her. As a Beast, I have an ability to become unembodied. It is what allows me to open doors of shadow and roam the other realm during their night.

I do not know the purpose of such an ability, but it provides me with another source of food when I grow tired of the animals available to me in the Shade Realm. The fish, rabbit, and deer in the Sun Realm have a flavor that I can only describe as weightless. I have found nothing compared to the flavor here in the Shade Realm. I dislike the Sun Realm because everything is smaller, making it uncomfortable to move around, also the dangers it presents, but the food is worth the risk. Since the start of the mage war, I have not ventured to the other realm, and I am missing those airy textures. Thinking about it now makes my mouth water. I shake myself from the daydream before I start to drool since there is nothing I can do to fulfill such a desire and again return my attention to Rayle.

My pup is still sprawled on the sand, pitying her position as the human in the bond. I let her have a moment, but I do not see the point of wallowing in things that cannot change. It is going to be painful every single time we join, so she can only learn to manage her mindset to make the pain seem less debilitating. It is all she can do. She chose this life; I am the Beast, and she is the human. We cannot trade places, only learn to act as one entity.

Rayle pushes herself up onto her elbows to stare at me.

'Yes?'

If I was any lesser being, her stare would make me uncomfortable.

"You have no pity for me at all, Irigiim?" Rayle asks, shouting to be heard over the wind coming off the sea.

'No. Pity will do nothing to assist you.'

She grumbles something, and from the flash of her feelings, I am willing to bet it has something to do with my unsympathetic nature. I have no clue why she thinks I am human-like. Most Beast are not prone to useless feelings such as sympathy or empathy. Those feelings do not keep us alive. Sure, we feel pain and loss, like I did when my sire was pulled violently into the other realm, but dwelling on feelings does not change circumstances unless you learn from them, so I really do not understand why Rayle thought I would have such notions toward her at this moment.

'Are you going to try again?'

"Yes, just give me a minute," Rayle gripes.

I may not have the sympathy my pup wants, but I commend her for not giving up despite the pain our joining causes. She knows, as well as I, that being able to join is an important part of who we are as a team. It signifies absolute trust in one another, ultimately strengthening us into a much more formidable pair.

Brushing sand from her loose pants, Rayle stands in front of me once more, and there is a new sense of resolve floating between us. It irritates her that I will not give her any sympathy, and thus is going to prove me wrong, and that she can complete the joining.

'You have nothing to prove to me,' I say, attempting to ease her turmoil.

Rayle frowns at me. *'Just do it, Irigiim.'*

I shrug my shoulders. It is the one human gesture that I picked up after my bonding. I like that it is multifaceted. It can either be construed as noncommittal or indifferent. I use it here because if she will not acknowledge the tension between us, then I will not address it. My pup is the one with the issue and she needs to resolve it on her own.

I stand, and if I have one complaint about the joining process, it is that Rayle is so much smaller than me; I really have to bow my front paws to touch my nose to approximately her center. My nose is bigger than she is, but I do the best I can. I look ridiculous, like a playful pup, and it is undignified. Shifting into my less substantial form, I pushed my nose into her.

Rayle grits her teeth and growls, like I would, but she does not resist my advancement. As I push more of what is essentially my essence as a creature, I can feel my pup's body change. Her muscles grow and gain additional strength, especially her legs. Her nails grow to thick points before returning to normal, and her senses sharpen. Tufts of fur sprout from her skin before being quickly contained, and her bones become more dense.

Now that she has not fought me or given up, the process takes less time than I thought. My pup lets out a gasp, stumbling a bit as she adjusts to the changes. I am tempted to instruct her on testing her new form, but before I can say anything, Rayle takes off running along the beach. Her speed vastly improved. It will never match my grace at an all-out run, but I can commend her on how far she makes it in a matter of seconds. For me, it is strange to feel the same sensation as I would in my legs while running, but I am entirely aware that it is not my doing.

My pup comes to a large jutting of boulders. She slows only marginally before taking a massive leap and making it all the way to the top.

'Whoo! Irigiim, this is amazing!'

'*It is exhilarating to run without hindrance,*' I agree.

'Wow, you can hear so much! I can tell how far out those gulls are. This is amazing!'

'*Mmmm.*'

I am happy that Rayle is enjoying herself, but not being in control of my body, and it absolutely feels like I should be, is unsettling and definitely something I need to get used to.

'Irigiim, we should try the conversion,' Rayle says.

'Yes, of course. This would not be a very good trial run if we did not explore all the abilities afforded to our bonding.'

Rayle snorts. 'Stop being so formal, Irigiim. We are not in the royal court.'

I do not know what she means.

'From what Eniila told me,' Rayle continues, 'I need to let go of the image of my body so that you can take control.'

'Gaipanii also warned I cannot be too eager, otherwise it creates tension and disrupts the process,' I say.

'What does that even mean?'

'Honestly, I am unsure, though we are bound to discover it here shortly.'

My pup takes a few moments to slow her mind. Joined as we are, it is much more difficult to keep our thoughts separate. Though we each have individual streams of consciousness, they commingle tightly in and around one another. Like Rayle, I believe I need to slow my thoughts, so that I focus on one task alone–which is not an easy feat with all the sounds and smells bombarding my senses. My pup pictures herself as a wolf, standing proud in obsidian fur and on all four legs. I take a similar approach and picture myself but the size of the lower-minded wolves.

I cannot pinpoint when it happens, but we must be in perfect synchronization because I can feel Rayle's spine change and the beginnings of a tail. Her front arms lengthen as her ears shift and become pointed. Fur starts to sprout over all areas of her skin.

I will be myself again!

That thought is a mistake.

The joy of that singular thought pulls me from our concurrent thoughts like the snap of a bowstring. Now Rayle and I are stuck in this half-phase that makes us both look hideous. It is a good thing no one is around to witness this humiliation. She, or I suppose we, have a partially elongated face and semi-pointed ears, her patchy skin does not match the full tail and disfigured form. We can undo this, but I shudder to think if that were not so. I would despise being permanently stuck in this half-way transformation. I shudder again. I do not want to stay this way at all.

'Well, if I wanted to scare my little brother,' she says, examining her body, 'then I think this would definitely go a long way in doing so.'

At least she is not upset. Especially since this is my fault.

'My apologies, it will not happen again. I shall be more patient this time,' I reply.

Rayle laughs at me, and we try again. This time we make the full shift, but it is not as smooth as it could be. I am trying to hold back, and she is hesitant to let me take over. When it is done, I give my body a good shake.

'That feels weird,' she comments.

'What?'

'The shaking.'

Hmm, that is interesting, since I have always found it a great way to loosen everything. In this form, I notice the biggest difference in my eyes. I can see colors I have never imagined existed. I look out over the water to see the sunlight play along the crests of the waves. It is beautiful.

'I understand now, Rayle.'

I sense her pleasure. 'I am glad you get to see what I see.'

'Gaipanii said that our eyes would trade as we shifted, but this is not what I expected. Did your vision change? Do you think my eyes are blue?'

'It did change. I could not see the colors you see now, and your eyes being the color of mine would make the most sense,' Rayle replies.

'We should find quiet water so that I may see for myself.'

'Concerned, Irigiim?'

'*No,*' I say far too quickly. '*Merely... curious.*'

Rayle does not believe me, I can hear it in her mental laugh, which I ignore and shift the topic.

'*Now, pup, let me show you what a real run feels like.*'

I howl and take a massive leap from the rock. With her additional energy circulating in my blood, I sprint faster than ever.

CHAPTER 14
CASTELL

Flickering tan and black-tipped ears blocked Castell's vision as he opened his eyes. The sun was streaming in through the book-sized window, making it possible for him to see the thin veins that snaked through Olke's abundantly large ears. She rarely lay on his chest, preferring to find a hole to curl in, but in this scrubby all-wooden room, his chest must have been the most comfortable spot. She probably missed her little burrow, comfy with the bits of shredded fabric to keep her warm. At least he wasn't an active sleeper and she could comfortably rest there all night. Castell reached up to scratch her head, causing her to wake fully and give a little chitter of pleasure.

"We cannot lay here and be lazy today, Olke. We have a war to join," he said, cradling the fox to his chest before sitting. She gave an enormous yawn and squirmed to be released. Luckily, she had indeed found a mouse last night for her dinner–the remnants still in a little pile near the corner–while he'd been in the common room, which would keep her full until this evening.

The benefit of having a small pet... less food consumption.

Tossing the covers, Castell stretched the sleep from his limbs and then splashed some water on his face to remove the night's pull from his eyes. After checking his appearance in the tiny square of reflective bronze, he made his way to the common room, leaving Olke to continue to snooze on the bed. He'd grab her before leaving so she didn't cause any problems for the owner and potentially get him kicked out.

There were a few patrons dotting the tables, all with sleep loitering in the corners of their eyes. He was in good company, at least. Placing a request with an older woman at the counter for his breakfast, Castell liked that she had a friendly air about her. The smile she gave him lightened a burden he didn't know existed. He crawled into the same place he had last night since it felt like his personal spot after the conversation with the soldiers. He thought about the day to come, and while he was sure of his decision to join the war, the act of going through with it was a milestone in his life. How would this change him? Would joining the Purist army strengthen him or turn him into someone he wouldn't like?

The barmaid gave him another sweet smile as she set a thick slice of fresh bread with salted fish, cheese, and a solid dark beer before him. The hearty breakfast was such a reminder of home, his mouth watered. Everything was so delicious. He devoured it in a matter of minutes, but he took time to nurse his beer. There was a heaviness to the drink that hadn't been in his ale last night. The beer coated his tongue with a delicious maple flavor, sliding easily into his stomach to fill him as if he'd eaten a whole loaf of bread. This was an extravagant meal compared to last night, but Castell considered that maybe the owner saved the best for patrons staying at the inn, leaving the less savory meals for the crowds. By the time he finished everything, the common room had cleared, and he felt like he needed to be rolled from the room and back into his bed.

Cannot let that stop me! Things to do!

When Castell managed to drag himself back to his small rented space, he found Olke already in his satchel, sitting so primly he had to let out a chuckle. She was a clever little thing, and he loved her for it.

"I would not leave you, girl," Castell said as he gave her head and ears a good scratch.

After giving his teeth a rinse with the ultra fine clay he brought from home, he looked around at his meager possessions and decided it was worth carrying it all with him. This tavern felt safe, but he also didn't feel comfortable leaving his sole belongings behind a flimsy wooden door. Still, it wouldn't do to carry around a massive satchel all day. Surely he could leave a few items of clothing with no actual loss. If it came to it, he could always purchase more. Ready, and with Olke happily settled in his pack, Castell stepped out into the bright sunshine.

Just like home.

Shading his eyes, Castell used his gift to help him locate the most eastern part of the city. It was one of the minor benefits of being a Weather Mage. He'd have to be disoriented to be completely lost. It was still fairly early, and while Brion likely wouldn't mind having him show now, Castell wanted to see a little of Whispering Flats for himself before potentially being thrown into the heart of battle preparations.

The city was in various states of disrepair. Citizens and soldiers had hastily rebuilt the more commonly visited establishments either by hand or by a harried Violet Mage. Most of the food sellers had decent buildings, but the cloth shops looked to have been abandoned for some time. Clearly new clothes were the least of the residents' concerns.

Maybe I was too hopeful about the clothes replacement.

The lack of cloth shops made sense. The citizens of a city in the heart of the years-long war would not be as concerned with the clothes on their back as much as they would the food needed to sustain or the shelter to keep them comfortable. Clothes could be mended more easily than people.

Castell turned from the obvious signs of war and followed his nose to a bakery. It was small, but there were honey cakes in the window. There was one particular traveling merchant that sold honey cakes when they came near Sun Glimmer each year and he always gorged himself on the delectable treat. His mother made honey cakes using the honey from rock bees and they were good, but secretly he'd always preferred the merchant's because the taste of the honey was better. Castell sighed. He didn't need to spend the money on such a delectable treat.

But there was always room for honey cakes…

After purchasing one of the sticky treats, he adopted a listless pace in the general direction Brion showed. Eventually, he stood before an impressive wall that had to be the command center as Olke licked sticky residue from his finger,

I wonder why I did not see this on my way in? There must have been a Mind Mage, but then why did I not feel the presence of magic?

Even now, the sights behind the wall seemed off, but he couldn't feel anything. His father was powerful, but Castell didn't think even he could manage a casting this grand without serious consequences. Maybe he could find out how it was done once on the inside. The fortress, of sorts, was the most impressive feat. It was not shiny or new, but it was definitely functional, and had clearly stood many tests from the enemy.

"What do you want, lad?" The guard asked, drawing his attention from the structure.

"Oh, Commander Brion told me to meet him here," Castell said.

The guard raised his brows. "That so? What's your name and where are you from?"

"My name is Castell, and I am from Sun Glimmer. I met Brion last night at the Pearl and Oyster."

"Wait here."

Castell clasped his hands behind his back and gave the second guard a friendly nod. He didn't have to wait long before the first guard and Giilo came into view.

"Well, there he is, the thinker! Glad you made it," Giilo teased, stretching out his hand.

Castell clasped his forearm and followed the mage into the camp. As soon as he passed the inner line of the wall, an explosion of activity pulled his eyes in every direction. Giilo had to come back and urge him forward, which was for the best, otherwise he'd likely have been rooted in the same spot until the sun fell. It was a lot to process for someone who lived in a community of fifty people. Chaos to him was a resident's dog disturbing a nest of rock bees and running all over the hills while being chased.

"No time to dally, Thinker, we just got news The Clerics are planning something big. Commander Brion is helping to plan the counter–attack and asked me to take you to the practice area and test your strength so he knows where to add you in the battle."

"I am to see fighting already?" Castell asked, moving but still trying to take in all the sights.

"What'd you think you'd be doing in a war?"

"It just seems so... soon? I mean, for someone who has never used their magic for fighting."

"No time like the present," Giilo replied. "Alright, here we are. Now, I'm a Nature Mage, so after a few initial tests, I'm going to throw some obstacles at ya. First, I need you to create a wind tunnel, as strong as you can, but also keep it contained, so it doesn't leave the confines of this field."

Castell glanced around the large open ground to find random plants sprouting from mud pits, chunks of metal, and something that had been set on fire. He'd be careful to avoid the objects as best he could, though a wind tunnel on fire would be pretty cool.

Taking a deep breath, the symbol on his wrist began to faintly glow. Castell flicked his fingers away from him–as if sending the magic out–and created a small wind tunnel. Not all magicians used a motion, but he'd used one since learning about his first casting and it stuck.

"Thinker, you gotta do better than that."

"You want it contained, this is how I do it, just give me a second," Castell snapped.

Giilo raised his hands placatingly.

With another flick of his fingers, the wind tunnel expanded up and out exponentially. His hair and clothes whipped as his satchel bounced against his leg, but he didn't stop. The cyclone connected with the clouds above, pulling them down, and the width of the swirling clouds easily overtook the forty-five meter wide practice field. The fire Castell planned to avoid quickly snuffed as his control of the severe winds tore at the littered practice area. Chunks of metal and dirt swirled with dangerous glee. It was not the biggest or most powerful wind tunnel he'd ever created, but it was the most he was willing to do in the provided space. The hardest part was restraining the winds. He could feel the swirl of air demanding to take up more than the space he was allowing. If he let go, this fortress would be shredded and he was sure that wouldn't win him any favors.

Looking at Giilo, he shouted to be heard over the wind, "Is this what you were looking for?"

Wide-eyed he responded, "Yeah, Thinker, that's good."

Castell quickly ended the casting. It was a relief since he really had to force the cyclone to behave contrary to its nature. He was always taught to work with the weather when possible. After such a casting, he felt like he could use a drink of cool clear water, but he was far from actually being thirsty.

"You said you were a powerful mage, but yeesh, that was impressive," Giilo said.

Castell shrugged. "I used to practice that kind of stuff all the time at home after one of the other Weather Mages taught me."

"You just did a casting that The Clerics would consider being of the highest levels of training. Creating weather patterns out of nothing… we've only got a few powerful mages like you."

"Oh." That put things into perspective for Castell. Now he understood why this war was such a fight for The Purists. "Do The Clerics have stronger mages in greater numbers?"

"Yeah, and it's why we've been slowly losing this war. We're a creative bunch, but they've got the advantage."

"I wish I'd known sooner," Castell replied, a frown burying the small bit of pride he'd felt at learning the strength of his skills.

"You're here now, that's what matters. Commander Brion's definitely gonna be able to use you," Giilo said.

"Did you want to test me more?"

"Not your strength, but how nimble is your response to the unexpected?"

Before Castell could reply, a vine hurtled toward his face.

CHAPTER 15
IRIGIIM

"*Thank you for letting me have one more day on the beach before we leave,*" Rayle says.

'*Mmm,*' I reply.

I hear my pup but my mind is on other things. The strange feeling I have is getting worse. The waters are frantic and the wind has become an unceasing howl, nothing like the steady breeze that should come from the sea. It is like the Shade Realm is responding to a breach that should not be happening. There is this unease that echoes along my connection to the other Beast. It is like this constant tingle running along my spine. I want to raise my hackles, but nothing else shows me that I should feel so cornered. My wild brethren describe it as odd tugs on their rumps or chests, but when they look for the source, nothing exists.

"Irigiim, are you even listening to me?"

'*Mmm.*'

"I am going to open a door to the Sun Realm, and I should be back in a while. Come for me if I have not come back by dark!"

I place a paw in her path. '*You will go nowhere, Rayle. It is not safe, and you do not know how many Sun Dwellers are out and could see you.'*

'Ah, so you are listening to me.'

'I am more aware than you think I am,' I say, bitter that she thinks so little of my mental capacity.

'Then what has you so distracted?' Rayle asks, fisting hands to hips.

I see no point in hiding it from her. If there is something wrong, she is going to find out, eventually.

'There is something wrong with the land,' I say.

'How so?'

I'm glad we are using mental communication. It comforts me because it makes her feel closer to me, safer. Not that I think anyone will overhear our conversation since this beach is empty, but with the way the land is acting and the experiences from my brethren, communicating silently makes me feel more in control and less anxious.

'I wish I could give you an exact answer, but the last few days I have felt constantly cornered.'

'Oh. Well, you hid your unease well. I had not realized you had been so bothered.'

'I did not wish to alarm you since you were enjoying yourself so much.'

Rayle sighs. *'Irigiim, you can always tell me–'*

'I know.'

Unspoken assurances float between us, waiting to be given purpose, but they remain adrift.

Hesitantly, I say, *'We need to go home. I will feel better if we are in a place that we both know well.'*

'Alright, Irigiim. I will not fight you. I am not stubborn enough to deny that the connection you have with the land is greater than mine.'

'Thank you.'

Rayle looks up the cliff to the plains. As narrow as the beach is, the face is too tall for me to jump without a good running start. Walking out into the sea for the distance I need will only hinder me, and besides, I refuse to step paws in the restless waves. There is a route to get back up there, but our travel will be far from the direction we actually need to go, and I do not want that. Either my pup can tell my feelings or we are thinking more alike. She suggests we walk along the beach toward Habiilanii, the great river that flows down the center of the realm separating the forest from the desert. I agree with the plan since I can easily cross; the water does not even reach a third of the way up my legs.

'We might as well make our way in that direction,' Rayle says. 'Want to give me a ride?'

I send her a feeling of amusement, knowing she prefers to walk, but we will certainly get further if I do most of the work. I can cover three times the distance she can, even at a sedate pace, so large is my stride. Though I appreciate her efforts to appease the worry haunting my steps.

I lower myself as much as possible, which means I have to sprawl my legs out wide and look absolutely unbecoming. It almost appears that I am dislocating joints, but it is the most effective way to lower myself. As it is, Rayle still has to use my fur to climb to reach the top of my shoulders.

Once I have awkwardly inched up to all fours again, I set my paws in our required direction and at a decent pace. It is a light run, enough that my gait is smooth. Any slower and my pup will bounce right off my back. That would be most problematic, as it could seriously injure her.

'How long do you think it will take to reach Habiilanii?' Rayle asks.

My size affords me the ability to travel several hundred human kilometers per day. We have spent our days on the beach at Tilkt Point, the southernmost spot in the realm, so we are at a minimum of six hundred kilometers from the great river. If I sprint some of the distance, then we will be there by sundown. If I really push myself, we can make it home by the evening of the next day.

I can push my body, but Rayle reminds me that exhausting myself will do neither of us good should the need arise for protection. She is right, but the undercurrent of her words tells me she is not quite ready to capitulate her sense of freedom to responsibility. Personally, I do not think she realizes the level of deference she will receive from her people now that she is a Stieti Tetsaa. I noticed it some in the markets of the Oasis, but I think she was too focused on shopping to pay others any mind. Plus, the residents of the capital are more used to seeing Beast and their partners for it to be something noteworthy. Back home, however, there are fewer Beast roaming the area and only a handful of Isokanii are actually bonded, so I have a feeling many will elevate my pup to a status she never dreamed of having. Still, I cede to running with intermittent sprints since we are at least heading in the direction I want us to go.

'What do you think is the first thing we should do when you get home, Irigiim?'

There are many options before us, and the truth is I never like options. The more straightforward something is the better. *'Honestly, I am not sure.'*

'Hmmm, well, we are protectors of the realm, so that would mean patrols, yes?'

'It is a logical conclusion. You might also consider training members of the Gahijett and Jaburshelee.'

Rayle snorts. *'What can I teach the warrior tribes when they taught me everything I know?'*

'I meant the young ones,' I say. 'They need guidance just like you did.'

My pup does not respond, but I feel that she is thinking about my suggestion. Despite our brief bond, I am stunned she often thinks so little of herself. Will I ever stop finding things that surprise me about her? I suppose that much of her insecurities are because of her rearing, but she is a Stieti Tetsaa now, and she has a much stronger will and heart than she realizes. Rayle would not have been able to bond with me if it were the opposite. The pain is excruciating from what she described. She had to accept death to bond with me, but at the same time, have a will to live. She tries to give me the memories, but many of them are hazy since she mostly remembers the pain. It actually impresses me because if all her mind could remember is the pain, but she maintained the will to live, it is a fine line she walked the night of our bond to be joined with me. Perhaps if I keep reminding her of the strength and perseverance she possesses, she will one day take my words to heart and not think so little of herself.

'Irigiim, thank you.'

'For what?'

'For sacrificing your long life to be bonded to me, for believing I was worthy enough to be a bond partner. I was terrified right before the ceremony started and all the way up to the point that you came, I doubted my decision. Then when I saw a Beast had chosen me, it strengthened my resolve. I will be forever grateful you saw something in me that I had difficulty believing.'

Her words touch me. Perhaps my feelings toward her are seeping through our link and making a difference. That is definitely not something she would have said outright a few weeks ago.

'I will always be here for you, Rayle.'

CHAPTER 16
CASTELL

Castell did his best impression of the tawny owls living near Sun Glimmer trying to adjust to the sudden dimness of the tent. It did nothing to help, unfortunately, as he was dragged through the entrance by Giilo, blind and unable to catch his footing. He heard a rock skitter and thunk into some wood. That was just perfect. The last thing he needed was to look like an idiot amongst the hive of activity, but maybe they were too busy to notice–he hoped.

"The Thinker is at least an Elder," Giilo said without preamble.

"We don't use that kind of language here," Liion growled, taking his anger out on the table with a fist.

Giilo rolled his eyes. "Relax, Liion. You're the only person I know who gets bent out of shape about the scale system. Besides, it's the easiest way to describe his abilities."

Liion looked like he was about to lunge for the man, and Castell discretely stepped to the side. Luckily, Brion wrapped an arm around Liion and spun him away from the table.

"Cool off, Liion. Come back when you can speak without anger," Brion commanded.

Liion stalked his way from the table, glaring at anyone stupid enough to make eye contact. A quick flood of light from the moving flap briefly blinded him. Castell knuckled his eyes. Would he ever see properly again? Adjusting his clothing, he turned his attention to the group of men before him. Several eyes scrutinized him, making him nervous. What were they thinking? What he wouldn't give to have his father's gift right now.

"I thought you might be powerful, but you've impressed me, lad, and at such a young age," Brion said. "Sadly, it might be too little, too late, especially if the intelligence is correct."

"Such a pessimist," Arlon chirped.

"Cut it out," Brion barked, as a small boy came to the table to hand him a roll of paper. "This is not a joke, Arlon."

Properly chastised, Arlon stepped away to busy himself with other paperwork.

Castell dashed his eyes around the table and then the tent. If this was the command tent, then he had unwittingly inserted himself into the midst of the men in charge of the Purists rebellion.

The gods must have really wanted me to meet these men.

He couldn't decide if it was great luck or not.

After reading the notes, Brion turned his attention back to Giilo. "He created a tunnel?"

"He did more than that! The cyclone was as wide as the practice field, as tall as the clouds, with some impressive winds, and he contained everything so as not to destroy the surrounding tents,"—Giilo looked at him—"the lad could have made it bigger and sustained it for a while."

"Just a few light breezes for hours at a time then Castell?" Arlo asked in a lighthearted manner, but there was definitely an undertone of marvel.

"How much water did he drink?" Liion asked, coming back into the fold.

"Just a couple of ladles at the end of our session, and I pushed him," Giilo replied.

The commanders turned to him. Unsure of what they wanted him to say, Castell blurted the first thing that came to mind. "I would like some more water if possible."

The three men raised their brows. Brion gave a sardonic laugh before admitting, "Lad, it's too bad you didn't come sooner."

"Why?"

"Should we really be telling him this? What if he's a spy for them?" Liion sneered.

Castell narrowed his eyes, but didn't defend himself. If this man would rather listen to his pessimism than believe what stood before him, that was his choice. It was not worth getting into an argument over.

"Kid, you working for The Clerics?" Arlon asked.

"No. How could I? My parents took me to live in a small mining village in the Day Crystal Quarries a year after I was born here in Whispering Flats. My father told me to come here when I said I was leaving."

"There you have it, Liion, the kid's on our side."

"Humph."

"Who's your father?" Arlon asked.

"Siggri Alderne."

"Well Apelgo's wine barrel, I'll be a drunk disciple," Giilo said.

"What?" Castell asked.

"Now that you say that name, I can see it."

"See what?"

"Siggri is my cousin," Giilo said, "and I haven't talked to him in... how old are you?"

"Six and twenty summers."

"Windrah's blessings... twenty-five years. I watched him walk away from this town before the fighting turned sour."

Castell raised his brows. He never expected to find a family so far from everything he knew as home. Before he knew it, Giilo wrapped him in a hug so tight he almost considered using his magic to put air into his lungs.

"I'd say that's providence, Liion. Any other lingering doubts?" Arlon teased.

Liion flared his nose and curled his lips at the man across the table.

"How is my cousin?" Giilo asked.

"Father is well and is happy with mother. I have a younger brother and much younger sister," Castell replied.

Brion interrupted, "We don't have time for chit-chat, Giilo. It'll have to wait for a pint at the pub."

"Right."

Clearing his throat, Brion said, "Regardless of Giilo's and Castell's connection, we're going to have to trust the lad. The sad truth is that we need the strength of his gift."

"Look, the only news of the war I had was from traders. I am here to help the Purists"—he looked at Liion, his biggest detractor—"if you don't want it, then I'll go where I'm appreciated." There was a tangible silence at his veiled threat. Castell might have grown up a pacifist, but that life was behind him and he would not let this one man's challenge determine his credibility when he'd clearly chosen a side to support. Liion undeniably had some unresolved issues. When no one objected to his bold statement, he asked, "So, what is going on?"

Arlon sighed. "We learned The Clerics are planning something big, lad. They're keeping the specifics hush, but there is a buzz of unrest throughout the ranks. That's what my spies have reported to me."

The four men looked at him, apparently expecting a reply. Castell had come to fight, to try to help in this war however he could. In an attempt to lighten the surrounding stress, he said, "Sounds like you need a powerful Weather Mage to tip the scales, maybe."

Arlon barked a laugh, Liion grimaced, Brion smirked, and Giilo clapped a hand across his shoulder. The gesture was jostling enough to make Olke stir. She pushed her nose and ears out of the pack to look at her surroundings, giving Giilo a sniff.

"What in the gods is that?" Arlon asked.

"This is Olke. We call them Crystal Foxes because their eye color matches the golden crystals we mine. They like to hide among the bigger gems and catch small prey. I found her as a pup, and she took a shine to me."

Castell scratched between her ears.

"What is she doing in your pack, lad?"

With a shrug, Castell said, "She dislikes being left alone. I tried to leave her with my family, but she followed me."

"Enough of this futile talk. We need to get back to the task," Liion said, a deep scowl distorting his face.

"Yes, of course," Brion conceded. Hunching over the map of the table, he continued, "We've held the bridge for so long, I doubt The Clerics will attempt to cross. I have a feeling that whatever they're planning, it will be from their side of the river. If it's as big as our intelligence suggests, then their biggest weakness will be a concentration on the castings."

Giilo stepped closer to the table. "What we need to know is numbers and where. Why couldn't the spies figure that out?"

"You know most of them are low in the system. We're lucky to have even gotten this much," Arlon said.

"Scrying still naught?" Brion asked.

"Yes, though, I keep trying. They'd be halfwits if they didn't have amulets, and we're certainly not dealing with anyone that stupid." Giilo said, discouraged.

"I may be able to help," Castell interjected.

Brion looked up from his position. Castell thought he looked a little like a vulture, ready to devour what scrap of an idea he had. These men were definitely starving for something good to happen.

"How?"

"I used to communicate with my father and brother at the quarries by trapping the vibrations of air while he was talking, and we were often separated during our work."

Liion narrowed his eyes. "I've never heard of someone doing that."

Castell looked him in the eye. He was confident in his abilities, even if the pessimistic commander was not. "Not to be rude, but you are not a Weather Mage. My specialty is atmospheric, and I learned the technique from one of the other Weathers at home. We always stood great distances to create bigger storms for watering crops, and we needed to communicate."

Liion deepened his scowl but said nothing to refute Castell's claim.

"So, what are you saying?" Brion asked.

"If you can tell me where to send the winds, it may be possible for me to get more information for you."

A rumbling disrupted their conversation, tossing each of them into a stumble. Castell glimpsed Olke's ears before they disappeared back into his satchel. At least he would know where she was and he didn't need to worry about her. In the distance, yips and whines dotted their way across the camp. The caw of the black river birds swelled and diminished as they too fled the area.

So many sounds brayed against his ears, but the next thing he heard was a *crack* as if lightning struck nearby. The earth yawned open, separating his feet. Castell sprang for solid ground, scrambling away from the crumbling edge. A tiny yip escaped Olke as she landed hard on the ground next to him. He worked to keep her inside the satchel as a desperate cry from Arlon demanded his attention. The man clung to the edge of crumbling rock, his face gone haggard and pale as his fingertips dug for purchase. Castell was about to crawl toward his newest friend to help when Giilo wrenched him to his feet. The earth still roiled, making it difficult to avoid the ever widening chasm.

"Kreshkt! They are destabilizing the earth!" Brion sprinted toward the entrance, shouting commands.

"Come on, Thinker. We gotta do what we can to distract them, give our guys time to mount an attack," Giilo said, once again pulling at his arm.

"What are we going to do?"

"I would think one of your unrestrained wind tunnels would do the trick!"

Giilo had a point. On unsteady legs, Castell made his way toward the river, dodging debris as it bounced along the ground. His arms flailed to keep him in balance as glass shattered all around him, adding to the chaos. How quickly something so reliable can break. Castell tapped into the magic inside him. He was going to severely hurt some people, but he also couldn't leave his chosen allies to be slaughtered. He still didn't like the idea of killing people, but he'd accepted the reality of his situation the moment he stepped onto the road. For the first time, he was using his gift for something other than the mundane. His past work with the Weathers at home had taught him to control and restrain his winds, but this was war and power rivaled prudence.

CHAPTER 17
TRIGIIM

A rumble wakes me.

It is not enough of anything to actually shake the ground, but I feel it nonetheless. I want to ignore the phenomenon and go back to sleep, except it never ceases. The movement I am feeling continues to strengthen. It is a constant vibration that can be classified as far from normal. This is not a ground movement like I have experienced in the past, where the earth rolls and dips violently. I remember what I felt under my paws before that happened. This is different, like fracturing instead of jagged shifts back and forth, but that makes little sense. Rayle is still asleep between my legs, and I hate to leave her exposed, but I need to know if the movement is isolated to our area or if it is something bigger. At least with her resting, I can hide my concern until I know more.

I shift to my less substantial form so I can be lighter and not wake my pup, but the change also gives me an advantage. I always feel more connected to the realm and other Beast when I am in my spectral body. That is not exactly the correct way to describe this semblance, as I am not a spirit–something the Isokanii believe exist–but it is the best description I could give to Rayle when she asked me more about this aspect of my being after bonding. It is such a part of me I never thought too much about it until she asked. Whatever it was designed for, it serves my purposes.

As soon as I shift, there is a cry from my fellow Beast, one of pure agony. The suddenness of it makes my form flicker. I crouch and cannot help but let a whine escape. There is so much pain.

"Irigiim, what is it?" Rayle sits up, my pain must have woken her.

'*Something is terribly wrong. Stay here.*'

I hold my spectral form this time as I step across the Habi-ilanii. What I discover scares me. I still feel the cries of pain from my brethren, but on the West side of the river, the rumbling stops. I move to the East side again just to be sure. Then, because I feel like I am being ridiculous and sensing things that are not real, I sit in the middle of the great river. I shift back to my more substantial form, and sure enough, the right side of my body feels this slight tremble while the left feels very little. The revelation is worth getting my backside wet. I probably need a bath anyway after the beach.

What can possibly cause this? I ponder the idea as I shake the water from my backend and move toward Rayle. I am concerned, certainly, but I am compelled to know what is happening to my brethren. Their cries of pain are more concerning than the rumbling. I never like to be uninformed about a situation, especially one as pressing as this.

'*Rayle, grab some of my fur and hang on, I am going to put you on the other side of the river.*'

I can find answers faster if I do not have to worry about losing my pup in the middle of a sprint, but I also will not leave her on the side of the river that causes my hackles to raise.

'*Irigiim, I can feel your worry. Tell me what has you so agitated,*' she says, still obeying my request.

'*I will tell you when I return. I need to venture closer to what I am feeling to gain understanding.*'

She wants to push me for more information, but is also wise enough to just let me go. I appreciate her restraint. I would rather explain everything I am feeling once and not waste time giving partial information now. It will only serve to make me more anxious and worry her. Those are two emotions neither of us requires at the moment.

'*Walk further West away from the river, I will find you when I return.*'

I take off at a sprint along the bank. North, toward the looming trees. The forest will slow me down a bit but not much. Even in the dark, I can chase a meal through these trees with perfect ease. Right now, the information I seek fills me with the same desire as the demand to fill a growling stomach.

My ears tremble, swiveling as I listen for sounds from my brethren and the other lower animals that live in the shelter of the Faakeae trees. I go maybe one hundred-fifty kilometers before sliding to a stop. The feelings from the other Beast intensifies so keenly, it shocks me into utter stillness. Pain from others causes me to whimper and clench my jaw. I was prepared to receive ill news based on what I felt, but the energy I am reading from my brethren leads down one trail. Hesitantly, I reach out to the nearest Beast. It is a He-Bear stuck in the middle of the river. He is far from me, and I am thankful I do not have to be any closer to touch his mind. I cannot physically see, but as connected to him as I am, I feel an instant awareness of his surroundings.

'*Brother, what is happening?*' I ask, but not in words. My wild brethren do not use Isokanii words to communicate, so our 'conversation' is scents, images, emotions.

'Run! Far, run!'

His deep rumbling voice echoes across our link and my heart races at the urgency the male conveys.

'Brother, please,' I whine, *'tell me what is happening.'*

'Pulling. Fight, but—'

He lets out a roar of pain and the connection is lost.

I whine again and sink to my belly, flattening my ears. I have this writhing perception that I am feeling pain–muted as it is–from the other Beast. We Beast are all connected, even after my bonding, but this is different, this tethering is unnatural. My legs shake, preventing me from running, and my heart is raucous. Everything is so very wrong. I know this feeling intimately because of my sire. Hundreds, and it has to be hundreds for me to feel the connection so categorically, of Beast being pulled into the Sun Realm, being enslaved, but they all fight desperately to stay connected to the land. To their home. I am lucky to be excluded from this phenomenal reaping, but terror still rips through me as the same emotions as when my sire was taken seize me—oppressively multiplied.

Rayle. I have to get back to Rayle. We are too far apart for her to sense what I am sensing, thank goodness, but I cannot leave her while this madness is taking place. I force myself to rise and run despite the terror governing my limbs. Distance between me and the He-Bear helps increase my speed, yet the echo of his pain still lives within my chest.

My world—and Rayle's—is about to change.

CHAPTER 18

CASTELL

Castell's cyclone whipped people, animals, pieces of buildings, and plenty of dirt in a frenetic spin as Castell directed the casting along the opposite bank of the river. He made several passes collecting the debris and making his winds wider before moving it away from the river. The terrified screams of the Clerics, barely heard over the roar of his creation, cut at his chest, making it difficult to breathe. He easily imagined the sounds of cracked skulls, twisted necks, and snapped spines. It twisted his face into a permanent grimace. Was he being needlessly destructive? Protecting those he defended? Was he simply trying to justify his actions? It was harder to decide with every passing second.

How long should he maintain such a monstrosity? Giilo hadn't given him any specific directions other than to defend. What exactly did that mean? It was such a broad command, and because of it, he felt more guilty about the lives he was taking. An enemy would disappear into the depths of winds and earth only to have another take their place. It was like they were lined up waiting to be the next to suffer for the cause. Was there really such an endless supply of magicians for the Clerics?

Have all those people really chosen to die for their cause or have they been forced into it?

He didn't want to know the answer.

Castell had been maintaining the casting for over an hour now, and the energy loss was finally wearing on him, a dry itch formed in the back of his throat. He could certainly sustain his casting longer, but Castell needed water to keep going and a break wouldn't hurt–from everything. The cyclone wanted to break free of his control for some time now. He could easily let go of his restraint and the tunnel of wind would happily whip about to destroy whatever lay in its path. Which meant it could hop the river and start doing damage to his allies' camp. It was an unlikely scenario since the river had a girth of over a thousand meters, but he didn't want to take the chance.

If he was going to back away temporarily to clear his mind, he might as well do some extra damage. Compressing the air from his wind tunnel downward with extra force, Castell cringed at the sound of bodies cracking under the current. Debris speared the ground. The thunderous sound briefly mutes other noises. Odd shapes jut from the water, creating eddies where none should exist. Even with his distance, he could see some of the sharp wooden beams and sheared stones claiming several lives.

A ravaged swath of destruction surveyed him, and he had to turn his face to keep the condemnation lurking in the back of his mind from overwhelming him. The ruination of people and land was a lot easier to be oblivious about when he was focused on his casting. Now, he just felt sick. Castell had done what was needed. He had followed orders. Except now, he finally understood why his parents had fled to become pacifists. He wouldn't label their choice as the brave option, but they at least knew what they wanted—not to see their home marred and violated—and stuck by it. The annihilation of life was something he had expected, just not this soon after arriving. It was a gut punch, and sobering. His parents wanted to protect him from this. No wonder his mother cried so incessantly after he'd announced his decision. He sympathized with his mother's feelings now.

Castell strode away from the river embankment. He needed a moment. Lifting the flap of his satchel, he peeked inside to see Olke staring back at him with wide, frightened eyes. No doubt she had felt the negative energy with it concentrated so much in one place.

"I am sorry, girl. This is why I did not want you to come," he said, giving the small fox a scratch behind the ears.

The ground rumbled, tilting him into an unsteady lurch. Castell glanced back to see the opposite bank lined once again with Cleric magicians, with their hands linked and eyes closed. Those that didn't have their hands linked in the chain had magicians touching their shoulders. His cyclone appeared to have done nothing. The bodies of the dead were stepped around and over. The sight of such disrespect made him sick. Would they never give up? Why did they want to win so badly? Was it so bad that people wanted to govern themselves?

Those not holding hands in the chain, at first glance, all seemed to be Mind Mages, the markings on their wrists glowing the same violet as the symbol in his father's wrist.

The ground rumbled again. What were they doing? He squinted his eyes and noticed that it was only the Mind Mages who were actively casting. Every other magician seemed to be just fuel to stoke the fire.

So much for a water break, he thought.

Wheeling back around to get close to the bank again, Castell summoned his magic, the symbol on his wrist glowed a vivid white as he reached into the upper atmosphere to gather frigid air. If he couldn't sweep the Clerics away in a wind tunnel, then he was going to freeze them in place. He'd known no one to be able to think or react well when it was cold. Maybe, here near the base of the cordillera, the people were more used to the cold than he, but the gale that he was about to set upon them would be difficult to ignore. Iced air whistled around him and across the river, spreading out like a vicious fan.

The wet air formed small clumps of ice on the surface of the water, and as the bitter current hit those across the bank, the magicians hunched in attempts to protect themselves from the onslaught. Light summer clothing whipped around frames that were turning unnatural shades of red, blue, then black as healthy skin turned raw from the drastic exposure. Soon magicians fell to their knees, but still they wouldn't let go of the person next to them. It created a toppling effect that had each magician falling until it reached the Mind Mages.

Leaving the other mages to spend time and energy to recover from the chill, he concentrated his stream of air toward the nearest Violet Mage, the magicians responsible for leading the casting. His winds encouraged the magician gripping the left shoulder to squeeze tighter, turning frost-bitten hands to a deathly white. If he refused to let go, he would either lose his fingers or be glued to the mage he desperately clung to.

What was so important that no one let go of the chain?

Castell narrowed his eyes. Definitely some resiliency prevailed amongst the Clerics, but in the face of a rimy wind, crystals of ice clinging to their garments, the magicians didn't seem as brave. This was starting to worry him. They all just needed to be convinced to let go. Castell turned his attention to the weakest part of the linked mages, their hands. Whatever The Clerics were doing, it couldn't be good, and it seemed the casting they were attempting needed the power of additional mages to accomplish it. He would do whatever he could to ruin the link, and any evil the Clerics wanted to perpetrate.

The ground, this time, shook so violently it pitched Castell forward, and he nearly ended up floating down the river with the chunks of ice. Unfortunately, the distraction was enough to interrupt his casting.

I cannot stop now.

Castell gritted his teeth and started the casting again, but the ground beneath him again pitched violently, this time shards of land distended as everything beneath his feet loosened, ready to crumble.

CHAPTER 19
TRIGIIM

My feet spray bits of moss and earth as I speed toward Rayle, leaving deep grooves in my wake. I care little that I am destroying the undergrowth or that sharp branches shred my sides, snout, and ears–all that matters is returning to my bond partner. Right now, I hate the forest. It is doing everything to slow me. My poor pup is probably terrified, alone, and unable to run fast. For as brave as she is, I make her dauntless. The worst part is she can't move as fast as me, and by now she has to feel the tremors. In the time that I have been gone, the tremors have leaked their way across to the west bank of the great river. Right now, I can only hope she is running as quickly as possible from the worst of it.

I am desperate to go faster, but I do not know how. Unless… unless I shift into my spectral form. I have never tried running while in that state, but desperation is a powerful motivator. I screech to a halt, sending a fan of black dirt out before me. My heart is threatening to leap out of my chest. I take the briefest of moments to compose my frantic–everything–so I can shift and move again in my eidolic state. My body seems to float. I am unsure how I will fare as I sprint to my desired location. I feel like I am running on ice, going nowhere fast. Except, the trees are speeding by me, and I am not dodging branches or leaves since they pass through me. I can now run in a straight line!

In twenty breaths, I once again find myself at the mouth of the river. I shift back to my solid form and start my search for my pup. I never understood why my sense of smell is always better when not in my spectral form. I take a big whiff of the air. Rayle's spicy scent tingles through my nose. My pup really loves spicy food, and it is constantly evident. Right now, I am grateful she loves spices so pungent.

Relief floods me as I notice her smell leading away from the mouth of the river. She lingered a little longer at the mouth of Habiilanii than necessary, but I will not lecture her for the pause. I told her to move, but to fault her for waiting for a little is gratuitous. She had recently woken, and I was in such a hurried state that it probably took her some time to sort all that happened.

A rumble pulses through the ground, actually causing me to stumble sideways. Not an easy accomplishment. What are those maniac magicians doing? How can they be so selfish to steal so many of my brethren? I growl. There is no justification for taking lives in pursuit of power.

I turn my walk to a trot, catching faint tastes of my pup's smell as I move in her direction. As soon as I find her, I am going to carry her as far west as I can. I may even wade into the shallows of the sea as a precaution. I do not know if the water will be safer than the land, but it is the only way I can put the most distance between myself and the great river.

I find Rayle perched in a tree about my nose height, which for her is a little over three and half meters off the ground. She smells like fear and sweat, but mostly sweat. I do not have to connect with her to know she is tired. She must have run for as long as possible to be as wet as she is. I lightly nose the branches she straddles.

'You did well, Rayle,' I say.

'I am sorry, I could not go any further. I used the last of my energy to climb the tree, but I was uncertain if that was a good idea or a bad idea, so I just went for it. At least these trees have lots of knots, unlike the ones at–'

'Rayle, you are rambling. Hush, you did fine. Climb onto my back, and I will do the hard work.'

She latches onto my ear, using it as a support so she can traverse the top of my head before sitting to slide down my neck. Rayle settles herself between my shoulders and clutches my fur in expectation of me running. I start walking. I will run at some point, but this will do for now. I am with my pup again, and I feel all the more settled for it.

My pace does not last for long. A deep rumble vibrates beneath my paws, and I shake my head as pain from hundreds of Beast echo through my mind. Whatever just happened, it is making the realm even more unstable. I decide it is prudent to run. I am unsure if I can make it to the western shores, but any distance is better than no distance.

'Rayle, make sure you do not fall off.'

This time I feel her use some of the thin rope she always carries with her to tie around a thick bundle of my fur. She will still have to hold on, but the rope will help her from having to cling in fear of falling.

'Okay, I am ready.'

I bolt through the trees, twisting and dodging as if I am chasing down an agile meal. A small part of me feels bad for Rayle because I still have not told her much, and I am doing nothing to conceal my fear, rage, and panic. She probably has so many questions. If we live through whatever is happening, I will tell her whatever she wants to know, whether it be facts or feelings.

The land shifts again, only this time instead of a rumble, it is like ice underneath the soft dirt and something is pulling at my solid footing. I make the mistake of looking down, losing my concentration and trip, diving headfirst into the forest floor.

Ouch.

I gingerly position myself so I can get my feet back underneath me without squishing Rayle. I lift my right paw and give it a lick. In my descent to the ground, I smashed up against the trees. I want to cry in pain; I have not hurt myself like that in many years.

'Rayle, are you okay?'

'My neck was a little jostled during the drop, but I will be alright. Are you okay, Irigiim?'

I am about to answer when I notice the echo of death clawing out at me. It pierces my mind, and I lose all else. I let out a lamenting howl. Rayle feels my pain, and she starts to cry. Back in the capital, I watched my pup burn a piece of paper from the corner. This wash of death feels similar. Achingly slow until the flames grow in size and quickly consume the entire page, reducing it to ash. My brethren, hundreds of them gone. All pulled into the Sun Realm to be slaves, lowly beasts, to the vile magicians that only crave power and control. Everything that makes us a noble race is ash in seconds. This is why magicians disgust me. I wish venom tainted my saliva so I could poison every last one of them with my bite.

I lower myself completely to the ground, whining as I rest my head between my legs. The loss of my brethren marks me in a way I will never be able to cleanse. I let my ears droop. The ache is so great that I cannot move, not even to protect Rayle. Physical pain is bad, I can still feel my paw throbbing, but this emotional pain is worse. I finally understand the phrase I have heard humans utter over the years, "to die of a broken heart". I watched a constrictor snake once. The process of the kill fascinated me at the time, but now I am the hare struggling, and the more I struggle to not let the emotions take hold, the tighter the coils become. How can I bear an ache like this? I feel my pup climb down from her perch. I am thankful she says nothing even as every ounce of my pain is being passed to her.

Rayle touches the side of my snout, resting her forehead there for a time. Eventually, her exhaustion catches up to her, and she falls asleep with a hand touching me.

Waking to a vivid red sunset seems appropriate. The echo of death haunts my mind.

So many lives lost.

I feel it as firmly as the ground beneath me. I am now a member of a species in danger of extinction. Beasts do not reproduce often because of our long lives. A pair might mate once every fifty to one hundred years. That is about to change. Just to keep us alive, my wild brethren will need to mate far more often. I only know of one other wolf bonded to an Isokanii, and she is too old to whelp puppies. I can only hope my wild counterparts will see this tragedy as an opportunity to work together to keep our species from disappearing from the realm.

I tilt my head, and my pup shifts in her sleep. I am numb to the idea of movement, so I close my eyes once more. Perhaps I will feel something again. I hope for something better, whatever it is, and I hope it will rise with the next sun.

CHAPTER 20
CASTELL

What was happening!?

Castell lurched from one foot to another, attempting to remain upright, but it was useless. He quickly found himself staring at the sky as the earth strained, roiled, and crumbled beneath him. Olke darted out of his satchel, clawing his chest as she scrambled up, wanting to be held, which he did, but there was an actual possibility that he could squish her amid trying to right himself. Every muscle in his body was tense from fear and self-preservation. He could only hope his small companion would be okay once this was over.

Along the edge of the bank, the Whispering River seemed to widen, stretch, and lose color. The earth was still brown with scrubby grass, but it looked as if a gray haze was covering his eyes. What was that? Castell remembered overhearing talks of the Clerics using Shade Demons as weapons, the hulking animal forms pulled from the Shade Realm to attack the Purists with devastating results.

Could that be... no... am I seeing the realm from which they come?

Just how many Demons were the Clerics trying to pull into this realm? Survival instincts kicked in, and he backpedaled from his position. Whatever was happening along the bank was not good, and Castell was willing to cut his losses, even if it meant incurring Brion's wrath. He would run as far and for as long as possible, live to fight another day. Blurs of arms and limbs told him he was not the only one to abandon his position.

It was a good thing he moved. Seconds later loud snaps, like when he was controlling air flows and there was a sudden drop in air pressure, made Castell trip, losing speed. He turned to see large obsidian creatures bursting into existence all along the bank. Towering animals in a variety of species that stood meters above his head. Wolves, forest cats, bears, foxes, and other predators shimmered into reality before him as the sun-bleached ground gave way to an ashen sand earth.

Another spike of fear gave his limbs extra speed. He did not want to face one of those creatures. Castell kept moving further from the river as quickly as his untrained body would allow. If anyone harassed him for being afraid, for not staying to fight the Demons, then they were trying to mask their own fear. The land was crumbling and massive creatures were appearing. How could he not be afraid?

A heavy rumble convulsed the ground and a loud pop like the threads of a garment relenting made his ears ring. A flash of brilliant light blinded his already unsure footsteps. Like a rock slide coming from high above the cliffs, the ground crumbled, starting at the banks of the river and racing toward him.

We are not going to make it.

The realization fell over him as heavily as the Beast now falling on his new comrades. Castell was sure he was watching the utter destruction of his world and he held little hope that running would save him.

Olke yipped in his arm. Fear penetrated every part of her, but most of all her eyes. He wrapped her in his arms, burying his face into her large ears. Tears slipped past his lashes. The ground vibrated under his feet as screams and the sound of breaking earth filled his ears.

Ama, Papa, Averek, Tiecia, I love you. I will feast with you at Apelgo's Halls.

"I am so sorry, girl," Castell whispered, curling himself over her. "I am so sorry that you are here with me, but at least we are not alone."

No sooner were the words away from his lips than he felt the ground beneath him give way and he fell into darkness, chased into its depths by the roar of Demons and shattering earth.

CHAPTER 21
IRIGIIM

I cannot believe what I am seeing.

Neither words nor feelings describe the horror before my eyes.

Half of the Shade Realm–the high plains, the beach, the desert–all of it is gone. At least from this side. It is difficult to believe I walked among the wheat stalks only a few days ago. Rayle and I stand at the edge of what was the Habiilanii. The great river is gone and nothing but depthless sea swirls below our feet. There is no beach, no transition, just solid ground with the roots of trees from the forest jutting from the rock, and the few not already lost to the water are clinging desperately with weakening tendrils. A sheared edge with water a few hundred feet below, choppy waves glitter all the way to the horizon. This is the new shape of the Shade Realm.

My pup said it was like someone took a knife and chopped haphazardly through the land. I agree. The jagged edge follows what I think is the path of the great river, like the water that flowed through it was a weak point in the land.

Now that I am standing here, I half wish I never got up. I should have been content to lay in the dirt beneath the trees to brood in silence, but Rayle insisted we travel back this way to see what happened. It is painful to see such a ruin. She made some convincing arguments at the time, yet looking at the obliterated land before me, I want nothing more than to go back to my spot and erase this entire ordeal from my memory. A part of me hoped that seeing the outcome of everything would help numb the pain of losing so many of my brethren at once, that knowing the magicians in the Sun Realm also most likely suffered major losses–fully deserved–would give me some satisfaction of justice. It does not.

I still do not want to believe I am part of an endangered species.

"It is almost night in the Sun Realm. We should cross and see the damage," Rayle says.

'No. I want nothing to do with the vile humans of that realm.' I growl.

"Fine, Irigiim, do not come, but I am going with or without you. Do not bare your teeth at me! I will be careful, and besides, it is our duty to investigate what happened. The Eastern half of the Shade Realm has just vanished, so what happened to the Sun Realm? The Mafelbno will want a report."

I hold back a second growl. My pup has a point. It *is* our duty as Stieti Tetsaa to see what happened. We are protectors of the Isokanii and this realm. I do not voice my agreement, but when Rayle opens a doorway into the other realm, I widen it and follow.

I stop with my rump still in the Shade Realm, shocked as I am by the change in the land before me.

It is dark enough for me to fully enter the Sun Realm, but the moon is only a waxing crescent which hinders the distance of my vision along with the huge bulges of earth that create sharp ramping points of cliff. Long curved spikes like a bear's claws curving to point toward the sky. It is as if the realms were shoved together and had nowhere to go but upward before settling to create the chasm between them.

I cannot jump the distance from here to the other side so wide is the gap, but the missing Shade Realm is on the other side. I know because I feel it, and if I close my eyes I can picture it. The high plains with its swaying grasses. The beach with its dark glittering shore and towering cliff faces. The desert with its ever shifting obsidian dunes. I have always known that the Shade Realm and the Sun Realm were nearly identical, but this change just proves it to me. If the Sun Realm had still been where it should, the high plains, the beach, and desert would be lambent with varying tints of golden hues—even in the dark—instead of the lustrous black. But there is no mistaking this part of the Sun Realm is completely gone, replaced by the nearly identical Shade Realm. Where it exists now is anyone's guess.

My beloved realm is unchanged, just misplaced. It should be connected to the forest (where my rump still is), separated by the wide smooth waters of the Habiilanii. Instead it rests separated from me by an unmendable divide. Sparks bloom and explode, sending showers of flame and ash into the air—energy. Magic energy. The bursts make my skin tingle uncomfortably and the scruff on my neck prickle. The only explanation I construct for this phenomenon is that the two realms are being demanded to fit together, and since each side is unwilling to touch the other, it produces these fantastic sparks of magic. I growl at the anathema. As far as I am concerned, nothing good ever comes of magic.

"What do you think is happening?" Rayle briefly sticks her hand over the edge of the chasm before pulling it back with a hiss. "I feel an uncomfortable tingle from these sparks. Is this the feeling of magic?"

'It is. I do not remember where I heard it, for it has been at least

three centuries, but the Shade Realm is the opposite of the Sun Realm.' I ease my nose toward the edge to give it a sniff and pull back when I get the sharp tang of fire remnants. *'So, as creatures of the Shade Realm we naturally negate magic for the most part. As you know we are not completely immune since we Beast can still be pulled into the Sun Realm. For as different as the realms are, they are still connected.'*

"I suppose it is for the gods to tell us," Rayle replies.

The response seems a bit lacking to me. Maybe she is waiting for more information before coming to a conclusion. I will ponder all of this further, but I know my partner relies heavily on her faith, so I do not push the matter with her.

"If the Shade Realm split and shifted, what happened to the other half of the Sun Realm?" Rayle asks, interrupting my thoughts.

It is a good question.

'I am unsure.' Giving another sniff, I add, *'I cannot smell anything but fire and sulfur and magic.'*

"It had to have been destroyed. It is the only explanation."

'It is an explanation.'

"What else could it be, Irigiim? The Sun Realm is simply not here. Did the gods allow the magicians to do this because they are angry with us?" Rayle asks the starlit sky. "Did we do something to deserve our land being shorn in two?"

My pup is actually hiding her emotions well, far better than I did with the loss of my brethren, but she is still traumatized and astonished. At least, those are the two human words I know to describe what she is feeling.

She sighs. "There is nothing we can do here. We should return home and see what we can do to help repair whatever damage has been done before seeing if there is a way to return to the Mafelbno."

WE ARRIVED at my pup's childhood home a few days later, far slower than we ought to have been. Rayle asked me to pick up the pace several times, but for once even her urging could not motivate me. I wanted to lay in the darkness and let it swallow me, so deep was my grief and despair, but my pup needed me so I moved, albeit slowly.

In her home territory there is a distasteful tension lingering in the air, it fills my nose and makes it itch. Fear and worry permeate everything. We barely emerge from the trees before Rayle's mother, father, and two younger brothers sprint from their home. I tune out the conversation since most of it is babbled words of joy and relief that my pup is still alive. I have never seen Rayle be touched so much nor allow that much from others. Her mother and father refuse to let her go, even after they have all settled in the dirt to speak of their experiences. What catches my attention is the update on those on the other side of the Shade Realm. Some significant changes have happened because of the rending.

One of my flying brethren brought the news before we arrived. Her sister Serrett is still alive, as is her new husband, and Rayle is pleased despite their sometimes hazardous relationship. I am quickly learning that you can still love someone and not want to be around them all the time. The worst news by far is the Mafelbno is dead, as are his three older sons. Apparently, they died in the Sun Realm attempting to stop the magicians responsible for this horrible act, and sadly it was a losing battle from the start. They crossed realms while the sun was strong, limiting their maneuverability and making themselves vulnerable. It was a desperate choice, but they were Stieti Tetsaa–what choice did they have?

Their death is significant. This comes as a surprise to me—mostly because I never stopped to consider the order of succession—that Rayle's father is now the leader of the Isokanii; and because Rayle's sister, Serrett, chose not to become a Stieti Tetsaa it now makes my pup the inheritor of the throne. Only a bonded leader can rule according to Isokanii law, which means her human mate will also have to be a Stieti Tetsaa as well. The male is typically the inheritor to the throne, but her father admits that with these drastic changes to the realm, he already has plans to change the law to allow a female inheritor as long as she married within two years of taking the throne. I hold back a grunt of disapproval at the caveat. My Rayle is more than capable of handling the rule of an empire on her own. There is no way for my pup to get out of it since she is the eldest child and a Stieti Tetsaa. Her only option to evade her developing responsibility is to refuse the title and train one of her younger brothers to follow in her footsteps.

I will not be shocked if this is the path she ultimately chooses. Rayle says nothing about the change to me, but I know she is not happy with the news. She mentioned to me on multiple occasions that she does not want to marry and has always been very specific about the responsibilities she will handle. Her dream has only ever been to be a Stieti Tetsaa. It is her one ambition in life. Perhaps with time, I can change her mind. Rayle does not want a throne, but it does not mean she cannot be what the throne needs. I will not force her, that is not my place, but I certainly will be a voice of challenge, so she decides with a clear conscience and not out of scornful emotion.

When words and mirth run dry, Rayle and I escape her home for a stroll through the forest. I am sure I could have attempted to put words to my thoughts and feelings, but I am content with a quiet stroll across the shaded loam. Everything else seems to understand the necessity of silence, and I will respect it. The creatures of the forest have little to speak about, and the winds taste different.

What a change life can bring at the snap of a bone. This is definitely not how I foresaw my life going. I stop to let the sun coming through a break in the trees shine on my face. Closing my eyes to let the heat warm my nose, I think about what is to be next. I am definitely unsure what the ensuing steps should be, a rarity for me, but I have an inclination that it is about to get incredibly stressful in all aspects of life. If there is one thing I can rely upon, it is that Rayle and I are not alone. We have each other. She will be my fresh breeze that leads to a prosperous hunt, and I will be her safe den where she can rest with ease.

REVIEW

I know this is the last thing you want to do after reading a good book. Personally, I would already be on the hunt for my next adventure, but reviews are important. It doesn't have to take long. One sentence with an honest star rating will do. Can you give me less than five minutes of your time? It's so easy. All you need to do is scan the code (psst, for digital you can click on it), and it will take you directly to the review page. If I could say thank you in person I would, so I'll leave it here instead. "Thank you, thank you, THANK YOU!"

REFERENCE & PRONUNCIATION GUIDE

Arlon (R-Lohn) - A leader of the Purist with a cheery disposition despite his circumstances. He is a trusted lieutenant under Brion's command.

Averek Alderne (Ah-Vair-eK All-Dair-nEH) - Castell's younger brother, and the middle child. Out of his entire family, he is the most angry with Castell leaving to go fight in the war.

Brion (Br-eye-ON) - The leader of the Purist. He first meets Castell at the Oyster and Pearl in the town of Whispering Flats.

Castell (Cass-Tell) - The main protagonist is unhappy with his lot in life. He refuses to spend the rest of his life chiseling rock to gather Sun Crystals. He leaves his family and the pacifist settlement of Sun Glimmer to join the war that has plagued the realm for the past twenty-five years.

Eniila (En-EE-Lah) - Rayle's instructor for the Ermyjek Ceremony. This instructor prepared her for what it was like to join with a Beast.

Ermyjek Ceremony (Air-meh-JeK) - The ceremony that calls a Beast of the Shade Realm to

REFERENCE & PRONUNCIATION GUIDE

bond with one of the Isokanii royal. The ceremony is merely a calling, and it is up to the Beast to choose to accept a partnership with the person.

Faakeae Trees (Fay-Kah-Eh) - The deciduous trees that make up the bulk of the forest in the Shade Realm. They are impressively tall, even the largest Beast can walk comfortably beneath their boughs.

Gaipanii (Guy-Pah-Nee) - The Beast partner of Eniila. He, too, gives advice to the Beast, who are considering a bond with one of the Isokanii royals. It is to prepare them for the shortened lifespan and the changes that will happen because of the bond.

Giiha (Jee-Ha) - Child Wind - Was the firstborn of Maker Earth and Lover Sky. He liked to play with the earth, using his wind to shift and shape the land into something different. His younger brother created the trees, and he liked to play with the winds to make the trees sway.

Giilo (Jee-Oh) - Castell's second cousin. Though, it's not known until later in his journey. He is a trusted lieutenant under Brion's command.

Habiilanii River (Hab-EE-Lahn-EE) - The name of the great river flowing between the forest and the desert in the Shade Realm. In the Sun Realm, it's known as the Whispering River.

Irigiim (Ear-ih-GeeM) - A wolf and a Shade Beast. He chose Rayle to be his bond partner so they could be Stieti Tetsaa, and to save himself from the same fate as his sire.

Jurana (Joo-Rah-nah) - Child Sun - She was the most beautiful of Maker Earth and Lover Sky's children. Lehlo loved her the most and so cradled her in the sky. Jurana loved her mother, but she wanted to be with her brothers and sister. She cried and her tears dotted mother with thousands of her sparkling teardrops.

Kaalak (Kay-lah-kK) - The husband of Serrett, and one of many Rayle's cousins. He is the second son of the second son of the royal family.

REFERENCE & PRONUNCIATION GUIDE

Kiiholee (Kee-Hol-ay) - Child Moon - The last child to be born the opposite of the sun. He did not have her beauty and Maker Earth and Lover Sky were going to destroy him. Jurana, though, protected her younger brother and spirited him away. This made her father and mother angry, but then Jurana shined her brightest and her light reflected off Kiiholee and his parents could finally see his beauty. They set him in the sky to always be the opposite of his sister.

Kikka Puthra (KihK-Kah Pooth-Rah) - Whoever named the row of stars believed it to look like a line of flowers. To Castell, it seems more like a splash of water against dry rock.

Kreshkt (Kresh-Kt) - An expletive used in the Sun Realm. It is meant to be difficult to say.

Liion (Leon) - He is the opposite of his counterpart Arlon with a grumpy negative disposition, but he, too, is a trusted lieutenant under Brion's command. Little is known about him other than he has had it harder than most in the war.

Mafelbno (Mah-Fel-b-No) - The emperor of the Isokanii people. He is also Rayle's grandfather, but she never refers to him in such a manner. This is not told in the story as it is not relevant to the plotline, but he attended Rayle's Ermyjek Ceremony and was proud of her becoming a Stieti Tetsaa.

Olke (Ol-Kuh) - The small desert fox that is Castell's companion. He found her as a kit.

Orttwin (Ort-Twin) - The owner of the Oyster and Pearl. An inn located inside the town of Whispering Flats. It is a popular location for Purists to end their day with an ale.

Ostiimii (Os-Tee-Mee) - Child Water - She was the second born. She asked her father if he would give away some of his land so that she could break up the monotony of the earth. Told no, she flooded the lands in outrage. Her tears formed the seas. After, her father gave her the space she desired, and she cried happy tears forming the lakes and rivers.

Pleasa Alderne (Plea-Sah All-Dair-nEH) - Castell's mother, a blood mage, and a gentle, kind-hearted soul.

REFERENCE & PRONUNCIATION GUIDE

Rayle (Ray-luh) - Irigiim's chosen partner. She is an Isokanii royal and a bundle of energy. She is also determined, strong, and adventurous. These are some reasons Irigiim chose her.

Serrett (Sair-Rehtt) - Rayle's older sister, with whom she mostly tolerates. She marries Kaalak with Rayle as one of her attendants.

Shurra (Shur-Rah) - The lithe fox that sits next to Irigiim at the wedding and wedding feast. She teases him for letting Rayle's energy affect him so much.

Siggri Alderne (Sig-Gree All-Dair-nEH) - Castell's father and a Mind Mage. He is not happy that his oldest son wishes to join the war, but he supports his decision.

Stieti Tetsaa (Stee-Eht-ee Teht-Sah) - The official title of those that complete the Ermyjek Ceremony. They are warriors and protectors of the Shade Realm. These warriors are the only ones able to travel to the Sun Realm to stop a threat to their world. They were unsuccessful in the war because of the time of day. Being sensitive to sunlight, they can only cross into the Sun Realm at night.

Sun Crystal - The crystals found in the quarries. They are a golden yellow color and mined for their value.

Sun Glimmer - The small town where Castell spent most of his life. It is a pacifist's haven.

The Oyster and Pearl - The name of the inn located in the town of Whispering Flats, that is a popular location for Purist fighters to unwind after a long day. The food is terrible and the ale could use some work.

Tiecia Alderne (Tee-Sha All-Dair-nEH) - Castell's little sister. She is several years younger than him and came as a surprise to his parents.

Tilkt Point (Till-Kt) - The place where Irigiim and Rayle spend a few days learning to become one and transition between forms.

REFERENCE & PRONUNCIATION GUIDE

Vaatla & Lindu (Vay-T-lah and Lin-Doo) - The story of the two partners was a classic tale of enemies. Lindu, a vulture, liked to steal the kills from the hunter Vaatla, for he was the laziest of all his kin. Because of this, the hunter was always hungry. In anger, Vaatla forever chased Lindu across the sky. Sometimes he was successful in killing the wretched vulture, but Lindu always found a way back through the gates of death to torment the hunter once more.

Whispering Flats - The town where Castell goes after leaving his home. It is where he meets a long forgotten cousin and joins the Purist in the war.

Acknowledgments

I have to admit that this part is tough for me. It's not that I don't want to show appreciation or thank those in my life, it's just that I struggle to find the right words to express my gratitude. I write entire stories and somehow cannot find the words to thank people. I'm indebted to them. My dream is coming true thanks to the people in my life, so I will give it my best shot.

I owe it to my Father for allowing me to see entire worlds when I close my eyes. I wouldn't be an author without being able to see things differently.

To my husband, who'd rather read police procedurals instead of fantasy, I won't consider it a betrayal. His hard work makes it possible for me to get lost in other worlds. I'll always be grateful for his sacrifice.

Addressing my editor and friend. Your challenge made me a better writer and I am thankful for that. You have my fealty.

Finally, to the loyal readers I have and who have been clamoring for another book since the first one came out. I know it's not the next in the series, but I promise that every day I'm getting one step closer to finishing. Hopefully, this novella will quench the thirst in the meantime.

About the Author

T.J. Fisher is the author of Heart, the first book of the Broken Realms Series. As a former mermaid, T.J. is a lover of all things fantastical and magical. After decades of watching humans write stories about her kind; she joined the fray and added her knowledge of magic to give characters a 'breath' of fresh air—so to speak. Lured to land by the love of a halfling and his endless supply of delicious culinary creations; T.J. now dines on the delicacies of enchiladas, breakfast tacos, milkshakes, and chocolate chip cookies. She may have lost her fins, but she still loves water in all forms.

Also by T.J. Fisher

The Broken Realms Chronicle

Magic's Daughter - Book 1

Coming Soon

Shadow's Son - 2025

Mage's Legacy - 2026

Sign up for news from the broken realms via **the fictioneer's inkwell**. A monthly report of all happenings in the kingdom. Become a fictionado today and stay in the know!

Made in the USA
Coppell, TX
24 February 2026

72302474R10083